JAMES

THE CIRCLE EIGHT

Beth Williamson *writing as*

EMMA LANG

Published by Beth Williamson
Copyright 2015 Beth Williamson

Edited by Catherine Wayne

Cover Design and Interior format by The Killion Group
http://thekilliongroupinc.com

For more information on the author and her works, please see **www.bethwilliamson.com**.

ISBN: 978-1-943089-03-1

**Join the Graham family as they make history in Texas…
Circle Eight: James**

The moments that define us are the ones we least expect to happen.

James Gibson spent his life trying to find his place in the world. The child of a feckless mother, abandoned as a boy, he was raised by his grandfather, only to lose him when he most needed him. Angry at the world, he struggles to find his path. Then he meets Catherine Graham.

Catherine "Cat" Graham is the hellion of her family, the youngest sister of eight children. She has bucked tradition all her life, riding horses like a man, wearing trousers, and refusing all femininity except for her long blonde locks. She isn't impressed by cowboy James Gibson, no matter how he made her toes curl when he kissed her.

When danger threatens both the Gibsons and the Grahams, James and Cat have to set aside their acrimony. Together they fight for those they love, and in the process find the other half of their souls.

TABLE OF CONTENTS

CHAPTER ONE

October, 1849

She stole his breath away.

James Gibson should have been watching the bride, but instead he watched her sister, Catherine Graham. She was wearing a dress. A goddamn, fucking *dress.*

He pinched the inside of his arm. Hard. He inwardly winced at the sting but he was able to suck in much-needed air. What had he been reduced to?

The youngest of the Graham sisters, Catherine was the hellion of the lot and until this moment he'd only seen her wearing shapeless men's clothing. The contentious female wore trousers all the time. How had her eldest brother Matt allowed that to go on for so long? She worked with the horses on their family ranch, the Circle Eight, but that didn't mean she had to go dress like a man.

But now she was dressed like a woman. Holy hell.

She was the tallest of the four sisters and stood beside the bride, Rebecca. The other two sisters, Olivia and Elizabeth, beamed from Catherine's right. Three of them had brown hair.

Catherine was the only blonde. He'd only seen her hair dirty, matted, snarled or up in a hat. Today it had obviously been washed and pampered and the golden locks shone in the bright sunshine like a goddamn halo. Someone had gathered her hair into a fancy twist at the back of her head, allowing the exceptional length to hang free down her back. All the way to her ass.

Sweet God almighty. Her ass.

He'd have thought seeing her in trousers would have told him she had a shapeless rear end. Not so. The clothes she normally wore were too big and hung loosely on her frame. The dress hugged her curves, tracing them down her long, lush form.

In another minute, he'd have to adjust his britches.

Then there were her tits. The woman was built for pleasure, more than a handful, those orbs of glory begged for a man's touch. She had those hidden beneath those shapeless shirts? How the hell had she managed that? And why hadn't he noticed?

The woman had literally disguised her feminine form from the rest of the world. He couldn't fathom why, but seeing her with all that nature gave her was enough to make him speechless with shock.

The wedding proceeded as if the world hadn't just shifted beneath his feet. He watched Tobias marry the woman who had owned his heart for years. The happiness between them shimmered in the air, reminding James he was there for his brother, not to ogle Catherine Graham.

Tobias cupped Rebecca's face and kissed her with a passion that roused the guests to cheer and whoop. James clapped his brother on the back and joined in. The Grahams surrounded them, a tribe of ranchers with wives, husbands and children numbering near thirty people.

The crowd moved toward the tables that had been set up for a wedding feast. The children played and ran around, squealing and laughing. The abundant sunshine brought the warmth of the fall day around them. It was perfect.

If only he could forget the tall blonde in the blue dress who skirted around the edges of his vision. She kept sneaking glances at him and that irked him. She had followed him around like a shadow the first time he was at the Circle Eight. Sassy and rough, she defied the definition of female with her ways, her mannerisms, and her insistence on being treated equal.

The second time he was at the ranch was only a month ago. He'd kissed her. It wasn't his intention, but it happened. And he hadn't stopped thinking about the feel, the taste, the texture of her mouth against his.

Shit.

James ducked away from the celebration into the shadowed barn. The relatively cool interior welcomed him. He puffed out a frustrated breath and ran his hand through his hair. As he walked past the stalls, a few curious horses poked their noses out in greeting.

The Grahams had prime horse stock. Even his new sister-in-law's gelding, Ocho, was a beautiful horse, if ornery. At the livery he and Tobias ran, the damn horse was forever trying to get a bite out of someone's ass. However, the breeding lines were impeccable and they'd started to sell the geldings for additional ranch income.

Of course, that led him straight back to her. The woman responsible for nurturing the foals, training the yearlings and riding the hell out of the mares and geldings. He heard tell she even rode the stallion they used for breeding. The woman was endless in her skills with equines, and for that, he gave her a grudging respect.

He didn't want to obsess about Catherine Graham. He sure as hell didn't need to be thinking about her body, her hair, her ass, her tits or her damn lips. That didn't mean he wasn't. She was too much. Everywhere and everything was too much.

Her sister Rebecca was the town healer, someone who aspired to be a full-fledged doctor who spent her time helping people. She was graceful and smart, elegant and respectful to others.

Catherine was the opposite of all that. She had him twisted up in knots and he barely knew her. He didn't want to get tangled any further. James needed to keep his distance from the Graham ranch and the youngest daughter.

"Why are you hiding?" Her voice cut through the silence.

He gritted his teeth to hold back the curse that threatened. "I ain't hiding."

"You're in a dark barn without a lantern or any company except for the horses while everyone else celebrates a wedding. I'd call that hiding." She moved toward him, a shimmering shadow.

He took a few steps back and she stopped. He could almost hear her smile.

"Why don't you like me, James?"

It was the last thing he expected her to ask. He struggled for an answer but his pride took over instead.

"I don't need to like you."

She sucked in a breath. "Your brother just married my sister. It's gonna be awkward at Christmas when you tell the family you hate me."

Then his stupidity hit. Hard.

"I don't hate you. I just don't think females should be doing men's work."

She chuffed a laugh. "You're a jackass." She turned around and strode out of the barn, her arms swinging.

He wanted to go after her but he didn't. No matter what he said, it wouldn't erase the words that had already tumbled out of his mouth.

Catherine was right. He was a jackass.

That son of a bitch deserved to get kicked in the balls. Catherine Graham wasn't a weak, simpering female who would sit idly by while a man disrespected her, no matter who he was. She would do well teach him a lesson he would do best to remember.

She stalked across the yard, weaving through the wedding guests. A few of them watched her warily. She wasn't the same wild girl she'd always been, but she wasn't someone to conform to what people expected from her. Cat was her own person and only answered to herself.

Well, she also answered to her brother Matt. And Eva, the housekeeper who was more like Cat's conscience.

Her temper curled around her like dark smoke, yanking her out of the happiness she'd experienced during the wedding. That smug idiot James Gibson. He'd stood there in the barn and told her didn't hate her, but he thought she should stick with female work.

Angry. Embarrassed. Annoyed. Frustrated. Any number of emotions flitted through Cat's mind. She had almost turned around to go back to the barn when a hand landed on her arm. She growled and turned to face whomever had stopped her, ready to let the words scorch whoever dared to touch her.

Her oldest's brother Matt's wife, Hannah, watched her with sympathy in her brown eyes. The angry words turned to ash on Cat's tongue. More like a mother than a sister-in-law, Hannah had practically raised Cat and her younger siblings for the last sixteen years. She was the matriarch of the Grahams and Cat had nothing but respect for her.

"Are you all right?" Hannah pitched her voice low.

"I'm going to punch him." She started to move toward her quarry, but Hannah held firm.

"This wedding is about Rebecca and Tobias. It's not for you to let your temper fly." Hannah never raised her voice. It was a spooky skill she had. Her own children only had to hear the first low tone from their mother and they all stopped whatever they were doing.

Cat was no exception. She blew out a frustrated breath. "I still want to punch him."

"Who are you going to punch? And why?"

Because he kissed me and acted as if it meant nothing.

"James Gibson. He's insufferable and I hope I never see him again." She sounded childish even to her own ears. If she heard her nieces or sisters talking like that, Catherine would remind them women don't whine. The man had turned her into a shrew. Another crime to lay at his feet.

"That might prove difficult since his brother married your sister." Hannah raised her brows. "You don't have to like the man but you need to be cordial. I know you have the good manners your parents, Eva and I taught you. Remember your family loves you for who you are. That's all you need in this world."

Hannah's advice diffused Catherine's anger. The older woman was right. James could think whatever he liked about her. That didn't mean it had to affect Catherine or how she felt about herself. She knew she was good at working with the horses and was a full-fledged ranch hand on the Circle Eight. Her family loved her and that was all she needed.

She'd worn a dress today because Rebecca asked her to and because Eva and Hannah made her a lovely garment. Eva had clapped her hands and whistled when she saw Catherine in the dress. For the first time in her life, she'd felt beautiful. She refused to let James take that from her, or the joy she felt for Rebecca.

Her mind made up, Catherine kissed Hannah on the cheek and her sister-in-law chuckled. "This is a special day."

Catherine laughed and walked toward the table to get something to eat. She wouldn't let James Gibson ruin everything for her. He would go back to town to his family's livery business and she would only have to see him on rare occasions.

If she were lucky, she could avoid him.

If she were lucky, she could erase the memory of his kiss. And his rejection.

The wedding wound down as the midday sun hit its peak. The children were down for their afternoon naps and the mothers relaxed on the wide front porch in the rocking chairs, sipping at cool drinks and chatting.

Cat leaned against the railing, watching as Tobias and Rebecca walked to the barn, hand in hand. They were headed to town to spend their wedding night in their new home. Rebecca had moved her things from the boardinghouse to Tobias's house two days ago. Since then, she'd been staying at the Circle Eight.

Now she was leaving again. This time she wouldn't be back on the ranch except to visit. It made Cat's heart pinch.

As if Rebecca read her thoughts, she turned and met Cat's gaze. After a whisper to her new husband, she kissed his cheek and returned to the porch. She held out her hand.

"Walk with me."

Cat smiled at her sister, the closest friend she had, and stepped off the porch. She took Rebecca's hand and they strolled toward the backyard, to the tree where their parents and Hannah's grandmother, Martha, were buried. It was a peaceful place, one Cat often escaped to.

The overwhelming excitement of the day had given way to a slow exhaustion. Cat still wore the dress because she wanted to make sure her family knew she would do anything for them. Even wear a feminine garment.

They sat on the grass beneath the tree and leaned against its trunk. Rebecca squeezed Cat's hand.

"Thank you for standing up with me."

Cat smiled. "That's the easiest thing I'll ever do for you. I was proud to be there and proud you asked me."

"There's no one else I'd want beside me."

The two youngest sisters had been close from the time they

were the tiniest toddlers. They'd shared a room for half their lives. No one knew more secrets, hopes and dreams.

"Are you happy?" Cat had to ask.

"More than I ever thought possible." Rebecca sighed. "I know he's not the perfect husband in everyone's eyes but he's the right man for me."

Cat scoffed. "Who cares what everyone thinks? If he's *your* perfect husband, that's all that matters."

Rebecca wiped her eye. "I miss you, Cat. Being here the last two days made me realize just how much."

Cat's throat tightened. She wasn't one to let emotions get the best of her, but this day had reminded her she still had them. The Grahams were close, but most days life was too busy to remember what was at the core of their beliefs.

Family.

"We're not little girls anymore. You're the Doc and now you have a husband, and maybe babies soon. Plus you've got Will to take care of." Cat's smile was bittersweet. "You found your path and I'm so happy for you."

Rebecca was the best healer in three counties. She'd taken over the doctor's practice in town. Although the retired doctor still lived upstairs in his office, Rebecca was the Doc. She had a bright future that involved her career, her husband and future children, and her husband's youngest brother who had suffered brain damage last spring. A perpetual child, Will was a ray of sunshine to every person who met him.

Now they were Rebecca's family too.

It was a difficult truth to accept for Cat. Her sister had been her constant companion all her life until six months earlier. Now everything had changed, but Cat stayed the same.

"I asked Tobias to give me a chance to say goodbye to you." Rebecca's blue-green eyes shone with unshed tears. "I'm having trouble doing just that."

Cat shrugged with forced nonchalance. "It's not like I won't see you all the time. Hell, you're only in Briar Creek."

Rebecca smiled. "I know, but it seems like something is ending."

"No, something is beginning. For you." Cat put her arm around Rebecca and touched their heads together.

They stayed that way for a few minutes, each lost in their thoughts. Cat was grateful for the few moments with Rebecca. Their lives were so different; it was hard to be alone anymore. No longer playing with the same toys or games, the girls were women with their chosen lives ahead of them.

"I don't want to be sad."

"Then don't." Cat got to her feet and helped Rebecca up too. "Go get busy with your new husband and find joy." She smiled with genuine happiness and hugged Rebecca tight enough to hurt.

"Love you, Cat." Rebecca raced off toward the front of the house, leaving Cat alone.

Life was simple when they were children, or at least as simple as life could be on a ranch in the wilds of Texas. Now they were walking away from their past and toward their future. Apart, but always together. The Circle Eight was the Graham family legacy. Matt always said their father had told him an eight turned sideways was infinity.

Cat would have to rely on herself to get her own life moving forward. She needed to remember the future of the horse breeding at the ranch was in her hands, whether or not Matt agreed with her.

"Catherine."

She whirled around to find James Gibson standing behind her. The annoyance at his dismissal earlier flared to life. He wouldn't disrespect her again. That was damn sure.

If only he wasn't so handsome with his thick brown hair, brown eyes and exceptionally wide shoulders. He was attractive, much more than she wanted to admit to herself. Her body temperature rose and it wasn't due to the heat of the day. The small hairs on her arms stood at attention as the air around them sizzled with tension.

He made her feel too many things at once and Cat didn't like being out of control.

"What the hell do you want?"

James shouldn't have watched the sisters as they shared a private moment. However, he'd been there first, after finding a quiet place to think. It wasn't his fault they didn't see him. That didn't mean he shouldn't have made his presence known, but they started talking before he'd decided to speak. Then it was too late.

The obvious love and affection between Catherine and Rebecca surprised him. He knew the Grahams were close knit, but these two were more than sisters, they were friends. He was envious of that. While he and Tobias had tried to mend the broken trust between them, they hadn't yet gotten past all of it. There was still an awkwardness that hung in the air, unspoken and unacknowledged, but still present.

Now to witness what true sibling devotion was between adults, James was a little humbled. He wanted that between he and Tobias. Will would be forever a child and his affection was something to cherish, but he would never be able to talk about anything other than what a child found interesting. Frogs, bees' nests, mud puddles and climbing trees.

James loved both his brothers, no matter what had happened in the past. Their grandfather, Pops, had raised them to rely on each other, but things had gone sideways after he died. It was up to James and Tobias to make their family whole again. They just hadn't gotten there yet. Now that his older brother had found the woman of his heart, they could focus on repairing what had been torn.

Catherine and Rebecca showed James a glimpse into what he could have if he kept at it. Now she was angry at him, which he supposed was better than following him around and annoying him.

She frowned at him. "I asked you a question, Gibson. What the hell do you want?"

"I don't want anything from you. I was fixing to leave and thought I'd be polite and say goodbye." A lie, but he had no other excuse he wanted to share with her as to why he was in the backyard at the Circle Eight. Particularly considering he'd eavesdropped.

Her gaze narrowed. "Seems to me you were here spying on me and Rebecca."

True, but he wouldn't admit it.

"I did no such thing. I'm a guest; is that how you treat guests at your house?" He was stepping deeper into the shit of his own making and he couldn't seem to stop his forward momentum. Foolish man.

She huffed out a breath. "I think I like you better when you're ignoring me. Or running away."

Catherine turned to leave. For some perverse reason, he reached out and grabbed her arm. It was the first time he'd touched her since the kiss. The fateful moment a month earlier when he lost his sense of reason and given into the primal urge to mark her.

He could still feel her lips against his, soft and surprised. She'd kissed him back, albeit with virtually no skill whatsoever. He'd been pleased to think he was the first person to kiss her. Then he'd remembered whom he was kissing.

Catherine set him on edge, made him feel uncomfortable and off balance. Today was no different, but the sight of her in a dress had made things worse. Even now, being within a foot from her lush figure, he fought the impulse to kiss her again. Or possibly run for his horse and get the hell out of there.

"Why you?"

She blinked. "What are you talking about?"

He took hold of her other arm, turning her toward him. Her form was curvy, but lithe and muscled from years of hard work on a ranch. A conundrum of raw sensuality and rough rancher. Innocence and experience.

Her gaze dropped to his lips and he knew she was remembering their kiss. His body hardened with an instant heat that flamed through him. He leaned toward her. She should knee him in the balls and run, but she didn't.

She licked her lips.

James covered her mouth. His body screamed at him to take, take, take, but he resisted the howling wolf in his chest and gentled his movements. He moved with care, soft kisses from one side of her mouth to the other. She made a sound of impatience in her throat and he smiled against her lips.

He lapped at the seam and she immediately opened her mouth and his tongue ventured into the sweet recesses. She followed his lead, dancing and moving with him. He groaned and pulled her flush against him.

That was a mistake.

James thought looking at her in a dress was difficult. Pressing against her perfect body turned him into a molten mess. He was hard as a stone behind his buttons and damned if his dick didn't push against the fabric, growling to be released.

He slowed his movements and pulled away a bit at a time until he kissed her forehead and stepped back. His breathing was as ragged as hers.

Her blue eyes were wide with surprise. He expected an identical expression on his own face.

"You kissed me again."

"I did."

"And your dick got hard."

His cheeks cheated. "It did." He sounded like an idiot.

"My nipples did too."

He couldn't help himself. His gaze dropped to her amazing tits and sure enough, twin points peaked beneath the blue fabric. His hands itched to cup them, his mouth to taste them, tease them.

"I'm all achy too."

"So am I."

She frowned. "I've had my education in the doings between men and women, but it didn't include how I'd feel."

He didn't know how to reply to that.

"I didn't think you wanted to kiss me."

He snorted. "I didn't."

Her scowl returned. "Then why did you?"

"I couldn't stop myself."

"I liked it. I don't understand why you didn't."

He blew out a breath and yanked off his hat. "I didn't say I didn't like it. You confound me, Catherine."

"Cat."

"I don't know what to do with you, *Catherine*."

They stared at each other, their bodies still humming with arousal. He would do well to stay in town at the livery, away from temptation. For once he was glad she didn't wear dresses every day or he would have to move to Oklahoma.

"What happens now?"

He shrugged. "I go home. You stay here."

Her mouth twisted. "What if I wanted to do more than kiss?"

He almost jumped a foot in the air as the shock rippled through him. Damn, but she was temptation in human form, tugging him toward a mistake he would regret. No matter how attractive she was, he needed to keep his distance from Catherine Graham.

"We can't. Besides the fact your brothers would tear me limb from limb if they knew what you just asked me, I got responsibilities and so do you." He kissed her quick. "As tempting as you are, this is the last kiss we got."

He forced himself to walk away. His back burned with what he knew was a scowl from the ferocious blonde. If he were a bigger fool, he'd turn around and return to her arms.

CHAPTER TWO

April, 1850

"Are you trying to get yourself shot?" James spoke behind him into the predawn light, certain she followed him. Again. "You need to get on home."

No response, which didn't surprise him. He felt her stare on the back of his neck, like an itch he couldn't scratch. Catherine still had no idea how to behave like a civilized woman. Instead she continued to wear trousers and rode a horse like she was in a race every moment of every day.

He rode onward, determined to do his job and ignore her. The last six months had been nothing but a struggle to continue to do so. She made that hard because she sought him out. With seven brothers and sisters, she knew all about competing with others and doing all she could to win.

He had volunteered to help at the Circle Eight for the next two weeks during the spring round-up, same as Tobias. They could have camped out at the site, but chose to ride there and back because of their younger brother. Will spent his days in Rebecca's office those days. Although they owned the livery and Will could spend his days there, it wasn't a good idea. He had occasionally wandered off or worse, gotten hurt. There wasn't anyone they trusted other than Rebecca to keep Will safe if Tobias and James weren't around.

Family was more important than anything, but Cat wasn't really his family. She was Rebecca's. He shouldn't have kissed her twice and he'd regretted it since. She'd challenged him, refusing to leave him be, so he'd done what he could to keep her quiet.

And he'd paid for that lapse in judgment every day since.

"Stop following me," he called out. "I got no time for nonsense today."

"I'm not following you." She spoke from somewhere behind him. "And I'm not nonsense."

"Catherine Frances Graham." He turned in the saddle and growled, refusing to let her see how startled he was to find her right behind him. She was as silent as a damn cat. "Go home."

She pulled her hat down low and glared at him. "You don't have permission to call me by my full name. Ever. Second, I'm on my way out to work the round-up. I'm not following you. Idiot." Cat galloped past him, leaving him to fume at how she'd once again turned around their interaction to make him look like a fool.

The woman rode like she'd been born on a horse, her smooth control of her mount more natural than walking. She worked with the young horses on the Circle Eight ranch. They entrusted the care of all the foals, yearlings, fillies and colts to her, which surprised him, but she'd been doing it since she was sixteen.

James grudgingly acknowledged the natural skill Cat possessed with the equines. Not that he would say it out loud to her. She would use that as a weapon to torture him, just as she'd done with every word out of his mouth.

It wasn't as if he encouraged her attention. Far from it. He didn't speak to her much and he sure as hell didn't seek her out. Or kiss her again. Not that he hadn't wanted to kiss her again. Every time he looked at her, he remembered her taste, her warmth, her heat.

James shook off the fascination with her and rode faster. The coffee he'd consumed sloshed around his stomach. He should have eaten too. Likely he'd have a headache and be more short tempered by the noon meal. If he were lucky, Rebecca had packed food for him in his saddlebags. He'd left his brother still smooching his wife, needing to escape the wedded bliss. Tobias would be along in a while, no doubt.

James didn't begrudge them their happiness, not even a little. He was twenty-three years old and wasn't in a hurry to find a wife and settle down. However, he also didn't know what he wanted to do with his life. He'd worked as a ranch hand, and now as a partner at the livery with Tobias. James had a path he'd yet to find. For now he was happy to be with his family and glad they were together again.

The pinkish orange of the dawn lit up the sky to his right. He was expected to be at the rendezvous point before seven. The sun rose around six forty-five so they'd be busy from the moment daylight was available.

The spring round-up was vital to a ranch. After a winter, they took stock of all the cattle and determined how many had survived the cold weather, gelded the young males and counted the calves expected. It was dirty, messy work and half the time they worked in muddy, cold conditions. Two weeks of back-breaking and exhausting days.

James had watched Cat participate in the round-up last fall. She'd worked alongside the men, never whining or complaining. The woman had grit and muscle, honed from years of working hard, if not harder, than her brothers. He didn't want to respect her for yet another skill, but he did, which made it harder to ignore her.

She had an uncanny ability to get under his skin, no matter how much he tried to ignore her. If only he hadn't kissed her, tasted her, pressed against her. If only she didn't wear trousers.

If only James didn't want to kiss her again.

❧

Cat hadn't been following him. Not really. She was on her way to the round-up same as him. James seemed to think she was obsessed with him. She wasn't. Not really.

Truthfully, she didn't know what she thought of him. He was the first boy, hell, the first *man* to awaken her body and make her feel like a woman. Since that day, he'd done nothing but think of new ways avoid her. Her body cried out for more from him, although she didn't even like him. It was obvious he didn't like her either.

They had been thrown together because his brother had been injured and Rebecca was the healer they'd needed. When he had arrived at the Circle Eight, she'd experienced a tug of attraction and fascination with the dark-haired cowboy. There wasn't any reason for it. She'd been around cowboys all her life. Cat couldn't pinpoint any particular reason for her ridiculous obsession with James so she had tried to avoid him. Then her sister had to go and fall in love with the eldest brother, Tobias, which left Cat and the rest of the Grahams stuck with the Gibsons, including the contentious James. He wasn't sad and grumpy like her brother Nicholas used to be until he'd found his wife, Winnie. James seemed to be simply unhappy. All the time.

It didn't bother her, or at least it didn't when she wasn't around him. He tended to snap at her or ignore her. She didn't care one way or the other.

Not really.

Who was she trying to convince? The man was darkly handsome and he had definite skills in kissing. Not that she knew a damn thing about it, but he seemed to, judging by how much she'd thoroughly enjoyed the experience.

She'd attempted to recreate the arousal he'd sparked, but it wasn't the same. Her hand was already familiar with her pussy and how to make herself feel good. She hadn't found the deep, throbbing ache James had elicited. Another reason she was frustrated.

If only he hadn't been avoiding her, she might have convinced him to kiss her again, and initiate her into the rest of the intimacies between a man and woman. Instead, he deliberately kept his distance.

The first bright slices of sunrise flashed to her left as she rode toward the meeting point. It was going to be a long day, even longer given how it began with James.

The stinker.

She leaned down over her gelding's neck. Paladin was a horse she'd raised from the time he'd been born ten years earlier. The first horse Matt had entrusted to her care when she was only eleven years old. His dam had been the strongest of their stock and the stallion in his prime. She'd groomed him, fed him, trained him and loved him as if he were her creation. In a way, he was. He had a blaze on his nose and a proud carriage so she named him after Charlemagne's warriors. She learned of them from the poem *The Song of Roland* that Hannah used to read to her and Rebecca.

She needed to escape her thoughts. Cat pushed her hat down

tight and spoke into his ear. "Let's chase the wind, boy."

As expected, he flew into motion and she clung to his back as if they were one. He loved to run. With his deep chest and unending stamina, he could run flat out for longer than any horse she'd ever ridden. It wasn't good for him, but he would do it because he loved it. And he loved her.

She laughed into the early morning air, her eyes stinging from the rapid cool air. She was happiest on the back of a horse or working with the young ones. There was nothing else she'd found that came close to that feeling.

Until James had kissed her.

Just like that, her joy at riding Paladin diminished. She sat up in the saddle, slowing his pace to a trot. In the distance she spotted the light from the campfire. Javier and Lorenzo had spent the night keeping watch over the calves and keeping the fire going. It had to be hot to keep the branding iron ready to use.

As Eva's sons, the ranch hands had been at the Circle Eight nearly all her life. Lorenzo had married two years earlier and Javier five years before that. She loved them like the cousins she never had. It would be good to see her friends.

She told herself to forget the man who rode behind her. The work that day would consume them. She was glad to be busy, then she didn't have to think about the man who crowded her thoughts.

Exhaustion crept through her bones. After three days of the round-up, her arms were numb and her thoughts addled. She returned to the Circle Eight hours ahead of the men. Matt had threatened to forbid her from working tomorrow if she hadn't left when she did. Cat was strong but she had a limit and she'd reached it.

To keep her thoughts under control she'd pushed herself beyond her limits. When she'd almost fallen into the fire, Matt had bodily put her on the back of Paladin and ordered her home.

Annoyed but grateful, Cat had never been so glad to see the familiar site of the barn and house ahead. It was late afternoon but not yet suppertime. If she were lucky, she would convince Eva and Hannah to help her heat water for a bath. Cat's muscles were sore and aching. She was usually the last in the house and the first out.

Not today.

Paladin picked up his pace, no doubt excited by the thought of his comfortable stall and feed. She rode past the yearling corral and almost made it to the barn when warning bells clanged in her head.

With a whispered apology, she pulled up hard on Paladin's reins and wheeled him around. Cat stared at the empty corral, devoid of the dozen horses that should have been frolicking. She swung around and raced for the barn, sliding out of the saddle before Paladin stopped moving.

Cat slammed the barn door open and ran passed the stalls, confirming what her gut already told her.

The yearlings were gone.

Her stomach clenched so hard, bile coated the back of her throat. Her heart hammered while her breath huffed in and out, choppy and uneven. She checked on the four mares with the foals and found their stalls empty as well. Dread wound tighter and tighter around her as she skidded to the end stalls, sliding in the straw strewn floor. She landed with a bone-jarring thump, scraping her hands. As her elbow cried out in pain, she got to her feet and glanced in the last three stalls to find all three pregnant mares missing.

Gone. They were all *gone*.

Panicked, Cat ran out of the barn toward the house, her arms and legs moving as if she were on strings. She felt out of control, spiraling like a crazed person. She skidded into the house, surprising Eva and Hannah. The two of them were obviously folding and ironing clothes. Eva's brows snapped together, her face full of concern.

"What is it, *hija?*"

"Tell me someone took the yearlings to a different location for exercise. Tell me the mares and foals are safely tucked away someplace." Her voice shook as shock raced through her system and her hands shook. "Tell me the horses are safe."

"Are you saying they're missing?" Hannah set the trousers down and walked toward Cat, taking her hands. "Take a breath and tell me what's happened."

Cat managed to find the words to convey what she'd found, or rather what she hadn't found. "You heard nothing?"

"Nothing unusual, no. When the children are eating breakfast though, the noise makes my ears hurt. We wouldn't have heard any noise outside except maybe gunshots," Hannah offered.

"I'm sorry, *hija*." Eva hovered by Hannah's shoulder, looking miserable.

Cat didn't have time for their sympathy. "The men are all at the round-up. Aurora is out at her shop, but she wouldn't have taken two dozen horses. Who the hell took them?"

She managed to run outside before she vomited. She shook with a thousand emotions as her eyes stung with tears. Who would take all the little ones and mothers? Someone who wanted to hurt the Grahams or the Circle Eight.

Or hurt Cat.

Her disbelief began to fade and be replaced by anger. Then fury. Her hands curled into fists. She would find out who took her horses and make them pay for taking from the Grahams.

She went into the backyard and pumped the well until cool water gushed forth. She splashed her face and neck, then drank. Refreshed, she took the canteen from the hook on the post beside the well pump and filled it.

Cat returned to the house and marched into the pantry. She took a sack from the pile and put some jerky, crackers and a jar of preserves. It would have to be enough. When she walked back through the kitchen, Hannah stood in front of her, hands on her hips.

"What are you doing, Cat? You've got us worried."

"When the men come back, tell them someone took the yearlings and the mares and foals. I've gone after them. I'm going to track them and get my goddamn horses back."

Hannah and Eva started yelling at once, trying to convince her to stay put until the men returned. Cat knew she couldn't wait. Every moment she wasted the horses got farther and farther away. She held up her hands to stop the other two women from continuing their tirade.

"I can't wait. I won't wait."

She grabbed the rifle perched above the door and a sack of ammunition from the basket that hung on the wall above little one's reach. She left the house, knowing they would follow her.

"Cat, please, you don't know who took them. You could be putting yourself in danger." Hannah's expression was tight with concern.

"I'm a Texan. Life is about danger. Without it, this land wouldn't be what it is." She tucked the rifle into the scabbard on the saddle, tied the sack to the horn and ran into the barn to grab a bedroll. Her earlier exhaustion forgotten. Cat was fired by fury.

Hannah wasn't about to give up. "Don't make me stop you."

Her sister-in-law was strong, and had been wrestling with young ones for fifteen years, but that didn't mean she could stop someone like Cat. Someone who spent her life on the back of a horse, working with animals, riding hard and working harder.

"You can't, so don't try." Cat secured the bedroll and threw herself into Paladin's saddle. "I'm sure I can track them. You can't move almost two dozen horses without leaving evidence."

She wheeled the horse around and headed north. It was the likeliest path the thieves would have headed, away from the other ranches, away from town, away from the Grahams.

Cat wouldn't fail at this quest. She would never forgive herself if she did.

CHAPTER THREE

James's hand throbbed in tune with his heart. The cut from the knife had gone deep enough it wouldn't stop bleeding. Matt Graham had sent him to the Circle Eight to have Hannah look at it. If she couldn't stitch it, James would ride another hour into town and have Rebecca doctor it.

He didn't like leaving the round-up in the middle of the afternoon but he couldn't hold onto anything. A one-armed man was useless during the fast-paced activities. He would be back out there tomorrow. He was sure of it. Another week or so and they'd be done. James could return to the livery and his life. Away from Cat.

She'd also left the round-up early. He hadn't seen her leave, but Matt had mentioned it. If James were lucky, he wouldn't see her at the Circle Eight. Both of them knew it was not a good idea to continue whatever it was that sizzled between them. That didn't mean he would forget it, but if he kept his distance, he could ignore it for a short time.

In the distance, he saw a lone rider riding hell for leather north. If he didn't know any better, he would have said it was Cat. He rode into the yard at the ranch a few minutes later to find Hannah and Eva shouting at each other. They stopped when they saw him.

This was not a situation he wanted to be part of. He held up his clumsily bandaged hand. "I, uh, needed a bit of stitching."

Eva mumbled under her breath and stomped into the house.

Hannah blinked a few times. "James."

"Yes, ma'am." He didn't like the look in her brown eyes.

"You hurt your hand?"

"It's a knife wound. Just need a few stitches. It won't stop bleeding." He dismounted and looped the reins around the hitching post. "I can head into Briar Creek to see Rebecca."

"No, no come inside." She tugged him forward and he wondered if he should have gone into town without stopping. Hannah pushed him into a chair with a little more force than necessary. Eva pumped water into a bowl and set it on the table, then set some on the stove to boil. Hannah bustled around getting a cloth and a sewing basket.

She sat down and started cleaning his wound with more speed than he expected. He hissed in a breath through his teeth as she probed the wound.

"Definitely needs stitches, but I don't think you did any permanent damage. It's deep but not wide." Hannah accepted some hot water in a cup from Eva and dipped the needle and thread into it. Hannah met the other woman's gaze and Eva frowned. "I need to ask you to do something, James."

He definitely should have gone into town. The hackles on the back of his neck stood on end. Something wasn't right.

Hannah didn't wait for him to speak. She held his hand and started stitching the wound. While he gritted his teeth against the pain, she continued.

"I need you to follow Cat."

He frowned. "Was that her I saw riding north?"

"Yes and she's riding toward her own death. Or worse."

James's brows went up. "That's serious."

"Someone has taken the yearlings, the foals and their mothers, and the pregnant mares. All twenty-three horses Cat counts as her own." Hannah continued to close his wound with tiny stitches while James tried to absorb what she told him.

He could barely take that information in. It was shocking. "*All* of them?"

"All of them. They're gone and no one has been here or left since this morning. The children will be home soon from school. The twins and Hope drive the wagon back and forth to town." Hannah's eyes shone with unshed tears. The twins were Matt and Hannah's oldest children and Hope was Nick Graham and his wife Winnie's oldest daughter. They were responsible young women but no match for their Aunt Cat. "Catherine refused to listen to Eva and me. She went off after whoever took the horses. Alone."

James's heart pounded. "Why didn't she wait for help?"

Hannah scowled. "Because she's a stubborn Graham who thinks she knows everything about everything."

He was familiar with that particular trait.

"You want me to follow her."

Hannah nodded. "It will be hours until Matt and the others are back. I know it's a lot to ask, but I am so afraid for her."

He should offer to ride back to the round-up and get Cat's brothers, but it would be several hours lost. Hannah was right to ask James for help. He was the only person there to follow up and possibly keep her alive. Cat wasn't known for her self-control or her restraint.

"Finish up then and let me get after her."

Hannah nodded, then sniffed. "Thank you. She's like a daughter to me and I can't bear the thought of her being hurt if I could do something to help her."

James knew about family, about doing anything he could to protect them. Regardless of how he felt about Cat Graham, she needed his help whether or not she wanted it.

"I will pack some food." Eva bustled around in the kitchen and pantry while Hannah worked on his hand. The silence pulsed with fear and anxiety.

"Do you have a rifle in addition to the pistol?" Hannah gestured to the gun on his hip. "And extra ammunition for that?"

The situation became very real in that moment. He'd had his fair share of scrapes in his life and been knocked around enough times to know how to protect himself. One thing he'd never done was shoot another human being.

"Yep. And ammunition in my saddlebags." He always had a few extra of everything with him when he was working. It had saved him on numerous occasions from going hungry and protecting himself from a snake or a coyote.

Eva set a canteen and a sack of food on the table. She took James's other hand. "You bring *mi hija* back to me, James Gibson." Her dark eyes pinned him to the spot. She was a formidable woman. "Don't come back here without her."

"Eva, you can't expect—" Hannah tried to stop her.

"Yes, I can. Don't think I forget who threw the fire on the house that burned." Eva shook his arms, her thumbs digging in. The intensity of her stare and the accusation in her voice burned him.

This wasn't what he expected when he arrived at the Circle Eight earlier that day, but it was apparently what would be his fate. There was no chance he would fail in this quest. His soul had a dark stain from what he'd done so long ago.

Never mind that he'd been a boy trying to be a man or that his brother ordered him to light the Graham house on fire for revenge. The Gibsons had done the Grahams wrong. Tobias had done penance by rebuilding the very house James stood in. James, unfortunately, had done nothing to right the wrong he'd done five years earlier.

Now was the time to change that.

Cat finally found the tracks after at least twenty minutes of doubling back again and again. The sons of bitches were smart, that was obvious. They'd wiped the tracks leading from the barn, possibly with a large branch, but they couldn't keep it up. A few miles north of the ranch, she found them.

She wanted to ride like the hounds of hell were after her, but she kept Paladin to a trot. The horse had to be taken care of and she wasn't about to run him into the ground. He trusted her and would likely ride himself to death if she asked him. Cat kept a steady pace instead. There was a creek in another two miles they would stop at for water.

If she were lucky, the rest of her horses were there. It was a long shot. If the thieves struck during breakfast, that fit the evidence given how dry the droppings were. They were already crusted over from the day's sun, which meant at least six or seven hours ago.

Simply stumbling onto the herd wasn't going to happen. Cat was going to have to do some hard riding to catch them. Matt was going to be furious when he found out what she'd done, not to mention Caleb, Nick and Ben. Her brothers were fiercely protective of their family, as was she. They couldn't expect her to sit around like a girl and wait for the men to save her.

Not a chance in hell.

The sun hung low in the sky as the day began to head toward evening. She was lost in thought of how to get her horses back on her own if, *when* she found them. The rider she hadn't heard coming was upon her before she could react.

"Catherine Frances Graham!"

She whirled around to find James Gibson. Her mouth dropped open in surprise. She forgot to chastise him for using her full name.

"What are you doing here?" she blurted.

"I could ask you the same question."

"Someone took my fucking horses!" She waved her hand at the tracks on the ground. "I'm going after them."

"I know that."

"Then why did you ask me what I was doing?"

"Because you're *one* person and whoever took the horses has to be more than one. Possibly half a dozen." James frowned at her. "I never took you for stupid, Cat, but going after that many men alone is stupid."

Her pride and her cheeks stung from the chastisement. "You've no call to insult me, Gibson. Go back home and leave me alone."

She turned away from him and kept moving forward. The nerve of the man, deciding to lord over her and hurl insults. She should shoot him.

He rode up beside her. "I'm not going anywhere without you."

He'd surprised her again. "Why the hell not?"

"Believe it or not, we're family. Gibson or Graham, we're part of the same clan and family never abandons family." He paused, his voice cracking. She didn't know the whole story of what happened between the three Gibson brothers, but now she really wanted to. "I made a promise and I'm gonna stick to it."

She puzzled over that statement and wondered if the man had decided it was time to torture her. "You regret kissing me. You won't do more with me even if you made my entire body vibrate. Yet you'll chase me across the landscape when I'm trying to catch horse thieves."

"That about sums it up."

She *would* shoot him.

"You're crazy if you think I'm going to let you ride along with me."

"I plan on bringing you home, not helping you."

She waited a moment before she spoke, her throat crowded with angry words. "Fuck you."

Cat knew Paladin was tired, but she urged him forward, ignoring James and his highhanded stupidity. As if she was going to listen to him. Hell, she didn't listen to her own brothers, why would she listen to her brother-in-law's brother?

"I won't go back without you." He caught up to her.

She took a second glance at his horse, impressed by the equine's stamina and performance. It was a fine animal.

"Then you're gonna be wandering out here for a long time because I ain't going back without my horses." She had raised each of them and damned if she'd let her babies think she abandoned them.

"This is stupid," he groused from beside her.

"Then go home. I ain't keeping you here." She couldn't push her horse for long. And damn that James Gibson, he kept up with her.

She could either ignore him or let herself be bothered by him. The horses were too important to her to let him endanger them. So she decided to ignore the man.

Unfortunately he didn't want to be ignored. Instead he kept lecturing her as they rode. The man could talk the bark off a tree.

"Would you just shut up?" She pulled Paladin to a stop, both of them breathing heavily.

James frowned at her. "For someone who claims to love horses, you're running that fine specimen into the ground."

Cat looked down at her mount and saw what she'd been ignoring. Heaving sides, frothing around the edge of the saddle and the pungent odor of horse sweat.

"Damn it." She dismounted in a flash, reaching for the canteen hanging on her saddle. With her eyes stinging, she poured water into her hand and murmured apologies to Paladin as he lapped at the liquid. She'd run him into exhaustion, exactly what she didn't want to do.

James, to his credit, didn't keep at her. He took care of his own blowing horse and waited while she let her gelding drink his fill. There wasn't much she could say to excuse her behavior. Not that she needed to.

"Why are you here?" She glanced at him.

He took off his hat and ran a hand through his dark curls. "Eva."

One word. That was all it took to diffuse any anger at him. Eva had been more than a housekeeper all her life. She'd been Meredith Graham's best friend and had comforted her children after her murder. She'd been the one to hold a frightened Cat when she had nightmares because of her mother's death.

Eva loved each of the Graham children as if they were blood kin. If she had asked James to go after Cat, then it was done out of love. How could she argue with the man if he'd been sent by Eva?

"Did she make you promise to bring me back?"

"Yep. Her and Hannah both. Felt like I was signing my name in blood." James slapped his hat back on his head. "I can't step foot on the Circle Eight without you."

"Were any of my brothers there when she sent you after me?"

He shook his head. "No, just Eva and Hannah."

Cat had a choice to make. One that might affect the rest of her life. She had respect for James and his horse. The man was a good cowboy. He'd shown that during the round-up. He was a solid man to have at her side while she chased the thieves.

"Then you and me are stuck together until we find those horses. Whether or not I wanted one, you're now my partner."

They walked the horses for the next half hour. James hadn't replied to Cat's offer to partner up. What he really wanted to do was throw her over her saddle, tie her to it and return to the Circle Eight. Then he could be done with her and go back to his life at the livery.

Selfish notion, but there it was.

He'd been surprised when she'd lost her annoyance with him at the mention of Eva. It was apparent the housekeeper was a huge influence in Cat's life and she afforded the older woman a great deal of respect. If only that meant Cat would simply go back home.

Instead she'd thrown a twist in his tail. Partners? He hadn't considered the idea of working with anyone in that way. Not even his brothers. Granted, he was now business partners with Tobias in the livery, but it was a situation that still wasn't easy. Yet.

Since his mother had dropped him at his grandfather's house when he was barely three, he'd always guarded himself against others. As a child, he did what was expected by Pops and Tobias, because James didn't want to lose his home again. When Pops died, James lost the anchor he'd come to expect in his life.

Then Tobias fell into a whiskey bottle shortly after, James and Will left home to make their own way in the world. Tragedy struck again when Will suffered an injury that damaged his mind. James was once again alone in the world and Will a perpetual child who was a joy, but not the brother and companion he'd been.

James had lost those people in his life he'd depended on, by choice or by circumstances. He guarded himself against trusting others. Now this loud, unusual and completely unpredictable woman wanted him to be her partner.

Not only that, he'd already kissed her. Twice. Enough to make his body stand up and pay attention whenever she came near. Her taste, her scent, her surprising appeal set him on edge.

Staying with her for an indefinite time was dangerous for many reasons. However, his gut told him he wouldn't be able to force her to go home. If he agreed to be her partner, perhaps her brothers and his would follow as soon as they heard Cat was gone and James had been sent to retrieve her. It was the best choice for a bad situation.

She kept whispering to her horse every two minutes. The gelding's ears would twitch and he almost appeared to be accepting her apologies for nearly running him into exhaustion. Her devotion to her animal was admirable.

"You plan on giving me an answer?" She broke the silence between them.

He grimaced. "I ain't got a choice here."

She snorted. "Then you aren't much of a man, are you?"

His pride stung. "I make my own decisions, but since I made a promise to Eva and Hannah, my choice is to keep watch over you. Save you from yourself. That's what a real man would do."

"I don't need saving, but I might need someone at my side with a gun." She peered at his saddle. "You got a rifle in that scabbard?"

He didn't know whether to take offense that she only cared if he was armed or be glad she was smart enough to want an armed companion.

"I got a rifle, and ammunition for the pistol too." He shook his head. "We won't need any of it if we head back to the Circle Eight now and let your brothers chase the thieves."

That was apparently the wrong thing to say to her.

Cat's expression hardened to stone. Her blue eyes could have been chips of ice. For a moment, James regretted suggesting they turn around.

"I don't need my brothers to chase the thieves. They stole *my* fucking horses. I won't let anyone take them from me." Cat sneered at him. "I thought you were different. You can damn well turn your sorry ass around and get out of my sight."

She turned, dismissing him outright. James should have used a different tactic to get her to turn around, but, hell, he didn't know how to talk to women. Certainly not one as unique as Cat Graham.

With a sigh worthy of any long-suffering man, he followed her. Somehow he would have to convince her to stop acting like a fool on a death ride and listen to reason. He didn't think Cat knew what reason was. She led with her heart and her gut, that was obvious.

She also knew how to cuss with the skill he'd seen from no woman in his life. He wouldn't ever tell her but he found it impressive. Women should know how to take care of themselves, in his opinion. Not that he spent any time around females. No sisters to speak of until Tobias married Rebecca last fall.

Rebecca was nothing like her sister. They couldn't be more opposite, but he knew they were very close. As the town's healer, the older Graham sister was unique amongst women. She was patient, kind and could fix up any ails her patients brought to her.

Not so for Cat Graham.

This female couldn't be more different than the one in the

dress he'd glimpsed at the wedding. As was her normal self, Cat was dirty from the work at the round-up with God only knew what stains on her trousers and shirt. She was as far from feminine as she could get.

Then why the hell couldn't he stop thinking about her?

CHAPTER FOUR

Cat didn't want to acknowledge his presence, but the large man beside her made that a difficult task. Why did he have to be such a jackass? He was a damn good kisser, but he didn't have any other redeeming qualities.

Except maybe his behind. And his shoulders. And his hands. The man had large, callused hands that might bring pleasure with just a touch.

Foolish to get lost in thoughts of a man who had just utterly disrespected her. She was more than simply a female, sister to the powerful Graham men. She was a Texan, a rancher, a horse breeder who had skills that far surpassed most men.

Cat had pride, perhaps too much of it. She also had dignity. James had chosen to ignore common decency and insult her by insinuating she needed her brothers to succeed at her quest.

It bothered her to admit he might be right. A little bit, but not entirely. She needed help to stop the thieves. If only the stubborn man stopped trying to convince her to go home. All he had to do was come with her to find the horses. If she simply ignored him he might follow her and do what she wanted all along.

Stupid plan, but what other choice did she have? If she continued to talk to him, she might end up punching him. Or shooting him. Neither would get her any closer to what she wanted. Manipulating him into doing her will wasn't something Eva or Hannah would condone.

Too bad they weren't there to scold her.

"You have stubbornness down to an art." He broke the silence.

She snorted. "I could say the same to you. How many times

have I told you I ain't going back without my horses, no matter how much you insult me?"

He was quiet for a few moments. "What are you yammering about? I didn't insult you."

She rolled her eyes. The man wasn't stupid, but boy he was stupid. "You told me to let my brothers do my duty. These yearlings, foals and mares are *my* responsibility, not theirs."

He apparently hadn't considered how his words might be insulting. "That ain't what I meant. Your brothers are a scary lot and, when they're armed, make a man piss his britches. You're tough, but you're no match for your four brothers."

She wanted to argue with him but, damn him, James was right. Her brothers were a frightening lot when they wanted to be. She'd never been afraid of them but she'd witnessed their fierce protectiveness all her life. Their support and love had cocooned her as a child, pushing her to rebel. To forge her own path and buck any and all expectations.

Cat continued to do the same over and over until it became habit. If Eva told her to wash her hair, Cat would smear dirt in it. If Hannah asked her to sit down and learn to sew, Cat went out riding. No one and nothing could keep her from being who she had to be.

Except horse thieves.

"No, but I can shoot just as good as they do and I can outride every one of them."

James frowned, then nodded. She wanted to hoot in victory.

"Riding hard and shooting straight won't get the horses back from a gang of armed thieves."

It was her turn to frown. "How do you know it's a gang?"

"You've been tracking the horses. You tell me." He pointed at the ground in front of them. "You see what I see."

She had focused on the smaller hoof prints. The youngest foals weren't shod and the two year olds weren't either. No one rode them yet and she preferred to keep them unshod on the soft sandy ground at the ranch until they were ready. She stopped and squatted down, gazing the jumble of tracks in the dirt.

Her stomach twisted as she counted, then recounted what she found. "Shit."

"That's about how I feel about it." James squatted beside her and pointed. "I've counted four horses with heavy riders on their backs. About seven horses who are full-grown but without riders. Another ten or twelve unshod yearlings." He ran his finger around one of the smallest tracks. "These little critters are running too hard for their size."

Cat's heart pinched. "Sons of bitches. How dare they risk my babies?"

"They likely don't know what they're doing with foals."

"That's obvious. If they don't kill the little ones, I'd be surprised. No matter what, I'm going to shoot them like dogs." Her hands clenched into fists.

"Then I get my turn at 'em." He sounded as angry as she was.

That was unexpected.

"Four men against two."

"You're not a man." He seemed happy to point that out.

"I've got a gun and a bad attitude. That's worth at least two men."

"That might be true."

"It's true." She got to her feet. "I'm happy to show you."

He smiled and stood, towering over her. Why did the man have to be so attractive and tall? Dark smudges sat beneath his dark eyes. He looked tired, exhausted even. She wondered if she were the cause or if it was the long days at the round-up.

She realized the sun wasn't down yet and the round-up went from dawn to dusk. Yet James wasn't there. He was here. Chasing her down. Suspicion made quick work of her attraction to the man.

"Why are you here?"

"I told you. Eva made me promise—"

She waved her hand in dismissal. "Not that part. Why aren't you helping at the round-up?"

He held up his bandaged hand. Rusty blood stains darkened the cloth. "Cut myself. Hannah stitched me up and then Eva asked me to go after you."

Cat wouldn't feel guilty he had been roped into Eva's scheme with an injured hand. At least that's what she told herself.

"Maybe you should go back and have Rebecca look at that."

He smirked. "You ain't getting rid of me that easy, Catherine."

While she wanted to tell him to stop calling her by her full name, she didn't. And she had no explanation why.

Shaking off the bothersome attraction to the man wouldn't be easy, but she was damn sure going to try.

The round-up was going well. They still had at least a week until they were done but no major disasters had happened. James Gibson had sliced his hand open so they lost him for part of a day, but if that was the worse that happened, Matt Graham would be surprised and grateful.

They rode into the Circle Eight yard as the sun was merely an orange crescent on the horizon. The blue of twilight lay ahead of them as night began to settle over east Texas. Matt was tired, but it was a good tired. He'd put in a solid day, as had all the men. Cat had stayed until the middle of the afternoon but when she'd nearly fallen into the fire from exhaustion, he'd sent her home. She was in quite a snit when she left, but she would get over it. He hoped she'd rested up when she got home. Eva would have tutted over her and taken the sting out of the dismissal.

His brothers Caleb, Ben and Nick, who had traveled in for the round-up, led the way into the barn, followed by Tobias. Javier and Lorenzo would keep vigil over the calves for another night as they had been the last three. The sounds of men murmuring to their horses as they rubbed them down filled the barn.

The hairs on the back of Matt's neck twitched and he glanced around the stall, seeing nothing. He stepped out and checked Cat's horse's stall. Empty. Foolish girl. She had pushed herself too hard and she needed rest, not to ride more.

He made quick work of feed and water for Winston and left the barn. His quick pace was fueled by his annoyance with his youngest sister. By the time he reached the house, he had worked himself up into a fine snit himself.

When he opened the door, he found the children at the table eating their supper. Over the din he spotted Hannah and Eva in the kitchen, their expressions tight. Now the hairs on the back of his neck were fully standing. His gut told him something was wrong and it had to do with Cat.

His daughter, Meredith, the older of the two fifteen-year-old redheaded twins, was busy bossing the rest of the children including her sister, brothers and cousins. He scowled at Hannah and jerked his head toward the bedroom and met her and Eva at the door.

"What's wrong?" He walked in and shut the door behind the three of them.

"Before we tell you, promise you won't be angry." Hannah's brown eyes were full of worry. He'd spent the last sixteen years looking at her beloved face and she rarely looked that scared.

Now his gut churned.

"What's wrong?" he repeated.

"When Cat came home she found the yearlings, the foals and dams, and the pregnant mares were gone."

Matt's mouth dropped open. "Gone?"

"Every one of them. She was frantic and angry. I told her not to go after whoever took them, but she wouldn't listen." Hannah wrung her hands. "I didn't have anyone to send out to the round-up to you."

Matt tamped his anger down. It wasn't Hannah's fault his sister didn't have the sense God gave a goose. Cat did whatever the hell she wanted regardless of the consequences.

"There are about two dozen horses missing and she went alone. Shit fire, why the hell are my sisters so hell bent on taking on the world without protection?" He glanced outside at the darkness that had fallen. "I can't even go after her because I have no idea where she went and I can't follow tracks at night."

"I sent James after her," Eva spoke up.

Matt took a moment to absorb that piece of news. "James Gibson?" He had accepted Tobias as Rebecca's husband, albeit with a bit of convincing. However that didn't mean he trusted the brother that actually lit the fire that burned their house down. It didn't matter if he had been fifteen years old, he was old enough to know it was the wrong thing to do.

Now James was the only protection Cat had against horse thieves. Matt might puke. He sat on the edge of the bed and put his face in his hands.

"Holy shit."

"I made him promise to bring her back alive." Eva patted his shoulder. "He's a good boy."

"Not by my reckoning. He burned the goddamn house down,

Eva. Remember, that's how Martha died."

Hannah's grandmother, Martha, had been in the house at the time. She hadn't died from the fire but from exposure due to her advanced age. Regardless, the Gibsons had wreaked havoc on the Grahams. Tobias had helped rebuild the house but James hadn't done a damn thing to make up for his crime.

"I don't blame him, so you shouldn't." Hannah was too kind by half. The woman had a heart of gold, which sometimes blinded her to people's faults.

"I don't trust him and I sure as hell don't trust him with my sister." Matt wanted to hop back on Winston and bring his sister home, but he also knew the folly of doing so. He could injure himself, his horse or possibly never find her. Texas was a big place. "Fucking hell."

Neither woman complained about his cussing, which was a bad sign. They were both as worried as he was.

Damn.

"I'll go after them." Ben's pronouncement from the doorway made the room quiet as a tomb.

Matt considered the possibilities. With round-up in full swing, they couldn't stop or they would risk not finishing in time. Sparing not one, but three people, would slow them down. However, stopping completely would affect every person on the ranch and the money they earned to keep them through the winter.

There wasn't another choice. Matt would have to send his youngest brother.

The sun had nearly set. A stroke of orange hung on the horizon but soon twilight would overtake them. Then full darkness. It would be unwise to continue in the blackness of the night and risk harming their horses.

James was bone weary. He'd been up before sunrise and worked until late afternoon. Then he rode for hours beside Cat. It had been an exhausting day and unless he stopped her, she might want to ride all night. His hand throbbed from holding the reins for so long. His gelding, Bernie, needed rest too.

"We need to stop."

"Huh?" She sounded as if she'd been asleep.

"It's almost dark. We need to stop for the night." He gestured to a large cluster of rocks ahead. "We can sleep there. It's tall enough to shelter us and the horses."

She was silent for a few moments. "I guess that'll do. Should we risk a fire?"

"With the height of the rock, it will block the light and the wind. We can risk a fire." He was hungry and thirsty. He hoped she had fixings for coffee because he could use some.

James hadn't spent time with this woman except when he was fighting with her. Or kissing her. What would it be like to spend the night sleeping on the other side of a fire from her? Knowing she was soft and warm and within arms' reach?

Torture. Pure torture.

He bit back a groan. He had to think about something besides her. That path led to trouble for both of them. And if any of Cat's brothers found out what they'd already done, he was in for some pain. Now if they knew what was rattling around in his head about what he wanted to do to her, he'd be buried in an unmarked grave on the Circle Eight.

"Did Eva pack food for you?" Cat pulled her gelding to a stop in front of the rocks.

"I've no idea what she gave me. There's a sack Hannah gave me and I sure hope there's food." His stomach remembered being mistreated and howled like a coyote. They hadn't stopped to eat once. The only reason they'd even slowed down was to give the horses a rest.

He dismounted and patted his horse's neck. "I'll see if I can rustle up some wood for a fire." James remembered the reason they were out there together. They weren't alone in the Texas wilds. There were likely armed men ahead of them by less than half a day.

He took the rifle with him.

After rooting around he managed to find a sorry collection of kindling and some dried brush. He walked a bit farther toward a ditch. In it he found one large branch. It would have to do and he sure as hell hoped he could bust it into pieces to burn it.

He dragged the branch back to their makeshift camp, stopping to pick up the kindling and brush. By the time he returned to Cat, she'd unsaddled both horses and they were happily munching the tall grass.

She eyed the branch. "You have a hatchet in that saddle bag of yours?"

"No, but I have a knife."

"We can spend the next four days sawing that monster log with a knife." She pulled a knife from a scabbard in her boot. "Maybe two days with both of us working on it."

A rusty laugh burst from his throat without warning. He couldn't believe it. Hell, he couldn't remember the last time he'd laughed, but damned if the crazy Cat Graham made it happen.

"We could just burn the end of it." He placed the kindling and dried brush around and under the end of the branch, then pulled matches from his shirt pocket. As he started the fire, Cat helped herself to the burlap sack hanging with his saddlebags.

She certainly wasn't shy.

"She gave you peaches?" Cat frowned. "Those are awful precious to her in the spring. She only has a few jars left."

"Are you jealous of the food your housekeeper gave me?" He told himself not to smile at her ferocious glare.

"I have to scrub the floors and the linens for two weeks to get even a bowl of these, much less a jar full." She narrowed her gaze. "You're going to split these with me."

He nodded with a straight face. "It's only fair."

"Damn right it's only fair."

James hadn't seen this side of her before. She set out the food like a regular female, giving each of them half a peach, a slice of jerky and a biscuit. Thankful she'd brought what he'd been craving, she ground coffee beans with a rock, then set the coffee pot on a small rock to wait for the fire.

She brushed her hands and got to her feet. "I gotta piss."

With that pronouncement, she walked around to the other side of the rocks. James stared after her, the crackle and pop from the flames the only sound in the deepening twilight. He didn't know what to make of Cat Graham. He'd kissed her, felt her passion, but he didn't know her. Her desires, her wants, her thoughts. She was a complete mystery to him.

She was as much of a stranger to him as he was to her.

Yet they would spend the next number of days together. Possibly a week or more. A warning echoed through his bones. It would be dangerous, potentially for both of them. Yet he was there, with her, allowing her to dictate what they did.

If only he hadn't cut his hand. If only someone hadn't stolen the damn horses. If only he hadn't kissed her. Well, no, he was glad he'd kissed her. She was kissable despite her rough behavior.

That was what worried him.

CHAPTER FIVE

Cat's stomach jumped as though butterflies danced inside it. She wasn't nervous. Usually. James Gibson set her on edge and she damn well didn't like it.

At the same time she did.

Life was full of the expected most days. James was the unexpected. Not that she wanted the damn butterflies in her belly or the ache he caused whenever he was near. At least she didn't think she wanted it.

That was the problem. Cat was confused and that made her angry. Combined with her fury over the bastards who took the horses, she was a twisted-up mess. Now she was about to spend the night a few feet from James.

The strange fire he'd built crackled while the flames flickered in the darkness. It was odd, but it worked. Using just the end of the branch would allow him to keep pushing fresh wood to keep the blaze healthy.

It was smart. She didn't know he was smart. What else didn't she know about him? Probably quite a lot.

After relieving herself behind the rock, she used water from the canteen to wash up. The horses seemed content where they were grazing. The night was calm, which surprised her as much as anything that day.

As she sat down to eat, she watched him without trying to make it seem as if she was watching him. He was stubborn enough to stick to propriety and what was expected by other people. Cat had left that behind before she turned ten. There was no point in following all the rules. Every one of her older siblings had broken with expectations and found happiness. Why should she be any different?

After she and James ate the simple supper, she put the plates and food stash away. He didn't have to know she put the peaches in her saddlebags. Cat resented Eva for bribing him with the precious fruit. At the same time, she knew that the older woman had done it out of love, and that made Cat's heart melt a little.

She untied the bedroll from the saddle and laid it out. That's when she realized it was missing the top blanket. One of the men must've taken it for some reason and left half a bedroll tied up for some unsuspecting fool like her.

Damn.

She glanced at James, who was currently laying out his own bedroll, complete with the top blanket. Envy at his preparedness sliced through her. He got the peaches *and* he would be warm. How was that fair?

Disgruntled and peevish, she laid down with her coat on top of her. At least she'd had the sense to stuff that in her saddlebags. She wouldn't be too awful cold, or at least that's what she told herself.

The night sounds echoed through the clear darkness, familiar and comforting. She let herself relax, despite her annoyance with whoever left the bedroll half undone.

Sleep claimed her and she fell into dreams.

James woke slowly, something niggling at him. He blinked slowly, recognizing the fire, the rocks behind them and the woman across from him. He'd spent plenty of nights out on the range with little or no company. Cat changed everything simply by being there.

A glance at the sky told him it was still the middle of the night. The stars winked at him from the velvet blackness. He closed his eyes again only to open them a moment later.

She'd whimpered.

That's when he sat up and looked at her. Not only was she visibly shivering, she was covered with only her coat. It appeared Cat didn't have a blanket. She hadn't told him, likely due to her pride. Yet the spring nights were still cool enough that a blanket was a necessity.

Stubborn woman.

He watched her for about two minutes before he got up. James gathered his bedroll and blanket and walked over to the shivering blonde. She would be angry when she woke up beside him, but it was worth her wrath to keep her healthy and warm.

He set the bedroll beside hers, then covered her with the blanket and crawled under it. At first he lay on his back, but her shivering didn't cease. With a groan of pure frustration, knowing he was going to regret his choice, he turned on his side and moved closer.

Closer still.

Close enough to touch.

He wrapped his arm around her waist and settled directly behind her. Her softness enveloped him, her scent surrounded him. She fit perfectly against him and he closed his eyes against the wave of need.

How was he supposed to sleep?

Cat stopped shivering within a minute and her body heat mixed with his, creating a cocoon of warmth beneath the wool. Despite the certainty he wouldn't be able to sleep, James closed his eyes.

The next time he woke night was still over them, the night peepers singing around them in a soothing melody. He was pressed up against her, an incredible, amazing sensation. James had never technically slept with a woman. Growing up, he slept with his brothers in the same bed.

This was very, very different.

He closed his eyes and savored the sensation. Considering she might shoot him when she woke up, he knew he had little time to enjoy it. He breathed in and out, reveling in the brief taste of closeness.

James hadn't spent his life being physically close to anyone. He didn't know how. When he saw the Grahams kiss, hug and sit on laps, he always felt odd. It was foreign to him. He couldn't fathom just walking up to someone and wrapping his arms around them simply because he wanted to.

Yet he could envision getting to touch Cat every day. She was soft and warm, but had lean muscles and a natural grace. Like her namesake.

A small sound emerged from her throat. He froze, hand on her hip, his dick standing at attention against her ass.

She shifted and pressed back, snuggling him farther into her softness. His entire body hardened into steel. His blood pulsed through him in a whoosh and he was completely, utterly awake.

"James?"

Shit.

"Huh?" He tried to sound sleepy but his voice came out strangled instead.

"Did you move me or yourself?"

"You were shivering." His excuse was ridiculous.

"Some idiot took the blanket from the bedroll. I was freezing, but you're so warm. Like having a stoked fire." She sighed.

He removed his hand, but she grabbed his wrist fast as lightning. "Where are you going?"

"I, um, reckon I should scoot back a foot or so." What he really wanted to do was move in closer, remove their clothes and feel her skin. He'd imagined how soft it was too many times.

"Don't you move," she growled.

He froze. "You know I have to."

"I know if you move, I'll shoot you."

He snorted and pressed his forehead into her hair. "I thought you'd shoot me when you found me sharing your bed...er, bedroll."

She pulled his hand up and before he understood what she was about, he was cupping a perfect breast. He closed his eyes and told himself he needed to move.

He moved his hand, molding and squeezing, learning the curve and shape. Her nipple peaked against his palm. He told himself to stop.

"That feels good. I want more. Do something else."

James didn't have any control. Snuggled up with the woman he'd been fantasizing about for nearly a year, he gave up arguing with why he shouldn't be doing what he was doing.

He reached for the buttons on her shirt only to find her already there. As she revealed her chemise, he reached beneath the fabric like a desperate man. When he found her skin, a shiver ran through him, making every nerve ending his body sing.

Exquisite.

Incredible.

James found the nipple that had begged for attention and pinched it between his fingers. She sucked in a breath and pushed her ass against his already-aching staff.

"More."

He kissed her neck, making his way up to her ear. As he breathed into the delicate pink shell, she shuddered.

"That feels good. More."

He turned her on her back and found her mouth. Their lips met together, fierce and scorching. While their tongues danced and rasped against each other, he moved to the other perfect breast. She was like no woman he'd ever been intimate with. Cat writhed and moved, her hip bumping his cock.

She growled and moaned, her untutored kissing quickly giving way to natural skill. She sucked at his tongue and he groaned into her mouth, imagining her amazing skills on other parts of his anatomy.

He lifted his head and she dug her fingers into his shoulder. "Don't you even think about stopping, James Gibson."

"I don't think I can."

"Good. Take your trousers off." She reached for her own clothes.

The next two minutes were a scramble of buttons and wiggling beneath the blanket. His heart galloped while his mind screamed at him to stop what he was doing.

There was no way in hell he was stopping now. No matter that he knew it was a bad idea. Both of them made a choice. Cat might not know how to do what she was doing, but she was a fast learner and strong willed.

By the time they were both naked, he forgot all the reasons he shouldn't be touching Cat Graham. Her warm, soft body pressed against his and he was lost. Utterly captured.

She ran her hands down his body and back up, exploring and touching. He did the same, ridiculously entranced by her female form. Cat made noises to tell him what she did and didn't like, which intrigued him. As if he needed to be more intrigued by the naked woman in his arms.

He kissed his way down her neck until he reached her breasts. As his mouth closed around a peak, he wished he could see the color. Light pink, raspberry red or, possibly, peach. He imagined the taste of her skin told him they were peach, sweet as the fruit they'd shared earlier.

She clutched at his hair, tugging hard enough to make his eyes water. "Holy shit. Yes, yes, yes."

He suckled at her, nibbling and laving at the sensitive bud. His cock throbbed against her hip, begging for release. He ignored his own needs and concentrated on her instead. She was an innocent by her own admission. He wanted to show her that intimacy between men and women was to be savored, not rushed.

Easy to think, much harder to do.

"I need. What do I need?" She scratched at his back. "Gibson."

He bit her nipple and she gasped, arching into his mouth. She pulled at his shoulder.

"More."

He spread her legs and slid his fingers into her slick folks. Jesus, she was hot enough to singe his fingers. So very wet, ready for him. He slid two fingers into her while he used his thumb to circle the hooded bundle of nerves. She groaned and spread her legs farther.

James shook, his entire body urging him to thrust into her, claim her as his own. He held back, needing to bring her pleasure. A shred of the gentleman he was supposed to be hung on by his fingernails. He restrained himself.

Cat, however, had other ideas.

"If you don't use that cock of yours in the next ten seconds, I'm going to make you."

He choked on his own spit, trying not to laugh. She was unique, beautiful and alluring as hell. James couldn't keep his lady waiting.

His lady.

Was she his? He couldn't focus long enough to consider what that meant. Instead, he slid between her soft thighs and pressed the head of his cock against her entrance.

"Yessss." She pressed against him. "Show me."

He slid in an inch at a time—slow, torturous progress. The sensation of sinking into her heat was utter perfection. He closed his eyes halfway in and grabbed for control before he came like a green boy in his first woman.

She grew impatient and pulled at his arms. He moved farther in, surprised to find no barrier to breach. He was seated deep within her body and the world once again shifted around him.

Sweet Jesus.

He had no idea what it was like to make love. He'd only known fucking with women who were only interested in his coin or his brief company. Nothing like this. No moment of his life had been as profound as this very second.

He withdrew then thrust into her pussy, the tight walls welcoming him, pulling him in. Pure pleasure slid through him. This was perfect. The most perfect he'd ever experienced.

His balls tightened and shivers of ache rocketed through him. She pulled at his shoulders, urging him to move faster. Who was he to argue?

He thrusted deep into her body, then withdrew and plunged again. And again and again. She met his rhythm, pushing up as he spurred in. They moved together as one, breathing in each other's breaths, reveling in the lightning snapping between their bodies. She moaned long and deep in her throat. An animal growl bubbled up from his throat in response. Cat scratched at his shoulders, his breath puffing against his lips and cheek. He picked up speed, unable and unwilling to slow down. Faster and faster.

"Oh God, James, I'm going to fly apart." She screamed as her release hit her.

Her pussy contracted him around him so tight he came, roaring as pleasure overcame him. He forgot to breathe. He forgot to think. He knew nothing but the woman in his arms.

The woman who had just shown him what perfection was.

Cat woke with a start, her body pulsing and throbbing. She had wanted to be intimate with a man for a few years but never met one worthy enough to do it. Until now.

James had snuck up on her blind side, showing her what it meant to be a woman. She didn't think he intended on that particular result, which was one reason she'd picked him. He was genuine, if sometimes contentious.

Now she'd crossed a line she could never uncross. She was

sore between her legs but otherwise, she felt good. Incredible. No wonder her brothers and sisters were so affectionate with each other and spent a good deal of time in bed together. Cat wanted to repeat the experience as soon as possible. Hannah had warned her that all the riding in her life might have breached her hymen, but it would not prepare her to be intimate with a man.

She'd been oh so very right.

She stretched and came in contact with the warm, hard, male body beside her. He lay on his belly, his face turned aside. She rolled to her side and pressed her breasts to his back. Although she always thought her tits were the bane of her existence, James had shown her they were much more than a pair of overlarge bumps on her chest.

What he did with his hands, his mouth and tongue would haunt her cravings for a long time. Perhaps years. At the thought of what he'd done, her nipples peaked again.

She almost rolled him over to restart the fun. He sighed and turned his face toward her. She studied him, fascinated by the opportunity to watch him in such a vulnerable state.

He had longer lashes than any man ought to, which was a damn shame because most females wished for them and had stubby lashes instead. Whiskers had sprouted on his chin and cheeks, dark slashes against his sun-toned skin. His dark brown hair was wild from sleep, curls and waves sticking every which way.

Cat touched one tousled lock. Soft as a kitten's belly. She found herself smiling without provocation. Good thing he wasn't awake to witness that piece of tomfoolery.

His eyes popped open.

She yelped in surprise and rolled, yanking the blanket with her. Cat peered at him, realizing far too late they were both still naked. Very naked. She pushed her hair out of her eyes and gazed at him. To her surprise, his dick hardened. Quite rapidly too.

"Does it always do that?"

He groaned and put an arm over his eyes. "In the morning, yes. When naked with a beautiful woman, yes."

She told her heart not to do a little jig. "Do you think I'm beautiful?"

"It's morning too."

She scowled at him, her pride smarting. "We need to get dressed and get moving. Sun is almost up."

Cat struggled to her feet then threw the blanket at him. She ignored his huff of impatience as she rooted around for her clothes. Naked and unashamed, she walked over to her saddle and pulled off the canteen.

As she washed up, she spent extra time on her pussy, the cool water soothing to the delicate tissue. Riding would be uncomfortable, but she wouldn't complain. Whatever happened beneath that blanket was her choice. She would *not* regret it.

After donning her clothes and cleaning up her things, she found James also fully dressed, sitting by the fire with a coffee pot on the reignited fire. Apparently having a branch in the fire kept the embers hot all night. Coffee was welcome to help her wake up and find control again.

Her eyes were gritty from lack of sleep. She sat across from him and wondered what to say to him. He was a stranger, but not really.

"What now?" she blurted.

"We have some coffee, pack up and start tracking the thieves." James checked the coffee, then put in a bit of cold water from his canteen to settle the grounds. "We also need to find fresh water. This won't last past midday."

He sounded matter-of-fact, as though they hadn't been naked ten minutes ago. As if his mouth hadn't been on her breast and his dick inside her two hours earlier.

She wanted to be as unaffected as he appeared to be. "If we keep heading north, there's a creek about ten miles ahead. I expect the rat bastards stopped there last night."

He nodded. "Then we should eat quick and get moving." He poured coffee for both of them into tin cups, then held out a biscuit and a piece of jerky sandwiched between the halves.

She accepted the food and chewed without thought, washing it down with the coffee. It was such a normal thing to do, but she felt anything but normal. This time their silence was awkward. She wished she could be as strong as her sisters to find a way to move forward without getting stuck in the past.

After eating the breakfast, they each slugged down another

cup of coffee before throwing the rest of it on the fire. He dragged what was left of the branch out of the embers. It looked like a giant writing instrument, as if some creature would pick it up and use it to mark the ground.

The silence continued as they saddled their horses and packed up the bedrolls. Her cheeks burned at the memory of what they'd done on that fabric and her body tightened at the desire to do it again.

CHAPTER SIX

James had never been so uncomfortable in his life. The two of them didn't know how to talk to each other, but they'd shared their bodies. Now they were off again, chasing a pack of thieves who'd stolen more than twenty horses from the Circle Eight. Danger ahead, danger behind, danger between.

How the hell had he gotten involved so deeply?

He almost wanted to turn back the clock and not cut his hand the day before. If he hadn't, Eva wouldn't have corralled him into chasing Cat. Then he wouldn't have known how she tasted, the sounds she made when she reached her peak, or just how damn soft her skin was.

"You regret it." Her voice startled him. It was like she heard his thoughts.

"Regret what?" He sounded foolish to his own ears.

"Don't do that. We're both adults, Gibson." She didn't sound angry, but sad.

"If you're talking about what we did under that blanket, I don't regret it for a second." The words fell from his mouth and he was surprised to discover he meant it. It had been his single most powerful experience with a woman. In fact, he could hardly imagine being intimate with another female and not comparing her to Cat.

Well, damn.

"For some stupid reason, I believe you." She shook her head, the blonde braid swaying against her back with the movement. "I guess that makes me the dumb one."

"You're not dumb, Catherine. You're smart as hell. Smarter than me. You're the one who figured out how to track the horses." He wasn't one to flatter. James was the type of man who stated facts.

"That wasn't hard. The tracks of the little ones are distinctive." She pointed at the ground. "These are from last night. They're not fresh, damn it."

"If you keep tracking them, we'll catch up. We can move faster than they can as long as we take care of our own mounts." He had been disturbed by how intense Cat had been the day before. Enough to put her beloved horse in danger. From what he knew about her, that never happened.

Until now.

Her jaw tightened. "I'm not patient."

"Huh, never noticed that."

Her eyes narrowed. "I believe you're funnin' me, James Gibson."

"I just might be, Catherine."

It was her turn to laugh and she once again, surprised him. Instead of a big, booming guffaw, she laughed like an angel. High, melodious as a bird song and so goddamn feminine.

He'd never heard her laugh before. When she wasn't being pushy and bossy, she was usually on the back of a horse leaving the world in her dust. Now she was here with him and he was slowly falling under her spell. James had told himself to avoid her. That hadn't worked out so well.

"We need to talk about what we're going to do when we catch them." Cat seemed very certain they would be successful.

James was hoping her brothers would follow and catch up to them before Cat got her hands on the horse thieves. It was a fruitless hope since there was little chance they would know where to go or make up the time.

"There are only two of us. We have to take them by surprise and sneak up on them before they know we're there." He'd decided it was their only option.

"Maybe. Sometimes riding in with guns blazing works too."

James scowled at her. "That's not a good plan."

She shrugged. "It's a plan."

"One that will get us both killed."

"Not if we shoot them first."

He ran his hand down his face in frustration. "I think our plan should use our smarts, not our bullets."

"Why can't it use both?"

"Because if I don't bring you back alive, I might as well throw myself in front of your gun right now." He took his promise to Eva seriously. Possibly more than the threat of what Cat's brothers would do to him if she died in his protection.

"Pfft." She waved her hand. "The bold win the day, not the meek."

"It's not meek to want to save your own skin. I want your promise we'll sneak up on them and find out how many men there are before we go in shooting."

She grunted. "That's boring."

"It will give us a chance to beat them with just the two of us. You said yourself there's at least four of them." He imagined trying to convince her of an idea she didn't come up with herself was like trying to chew rocks. Painful and pointless.

"One Graham is worth five or six men."

James wanted to howl. He had to change his tactic. "I reckon that's true. If we want to save the horses, though, we need to be more careful."

She was silent for a minute. "Damn, you're good."

He smiled. "So are you."

"You're right about the horses. If the bullets start flying, they'll panic and run right into them. I can't lose my babies, James." Her voice dropped low and rough. "I raised every one of them from the time they were born. They're scared and I'm sure they're wondering where I am."

He heard true emotion in her voice, and vulnerability. Very un-Cat-like. He had always assumed she was as strong as the face she showed the world. James was pleased to discover the human side to this force of nature.

"If you raised them, they're tough as hell and strong. I doubt they're as scared as you are."

She didn't reply.

"We'll find them." He didn't know if he was reassuring himself or her.

The sun was barely a wink on the horizon when Ben Graham saddled his horse. He was glad Matt had agreed to send him after

Cat. The truth was, he would have gone anyway. She was his sister and his friend. The only sibling who didn't try to change him and accepted him for who he was today, not who he'd been when he was five.

She was simply there. A friend, a sister, a human being. Cat was as free as she wanted to be and he envied her for that. She did as she wanted, no matter what anyone else said or thought. Ben had tried to fade from view until he was unseen and unheard.

It didn't work with the Grahams very well. Between Eva's mothering and Hannah's concerns, not to mention the nieces and nephews, brothers and sisters, and their spouses, there was no peace. It was cacophony every day, just as he remembered when he was a little boy. Before the dark time.

Before he learned how to disappear from his own skin.

Before he became invisible.

Ben led his horse out of the barn and checked to be sure he had all he needed. Since he didn't have any idea where Cat was or what direction she headed, it might be some time before he found her and James.

James Gibson was another person who had accepted Ben for who he'd become, not who he'd been. They'd met when they were young men and found common ground. James hadn't known Ben before he'd been kidnapped, which turned out to be a good thing. Ben wouldn't call them friends, but they had remained respectful of each other.

Ben was sure James would do his best to keep Cat safe. If he'd caught up to her. She was a damn good horseman, best in the family to be certain. Her horse, Paladin, was a beautiful animal who could outrun every other horse in their stable.

Ben wouldn't come home until he found them. No matter what Matt thought or how much Eva lectured him on returning to the Circle Eight.

After all, Ben knew how to be invisible.

As the afternoon arrived, Cat and James had somehow moved past the awkward moments from the morning. Perhaps it was his logic in the face of her passion to get her horses back. His ideas made sense, although she wasn't used to listening to other people.

She always had to prove herself in a family of strong men and women. No one gave any respect without action. Cat was the youngest girl and when Benjy was gone for five years, she was lonely in the midst of a crazy life. Even with Rebecca as her closest sibling, Cat felt adrift.

When Benjy finally returned, he wasn't the same and neither was their relationship. She was about the only person he talked to aside from their oldest sister, Olivia, but he was somewhere else. It was hard to explain to people, but even if he was home, his mind and his heart had never returned to the Circle Eight.

That was when she took to riding the horses and wearing trousers. It was freedom, it was respect for her burgeoning skills as a horsewoman. She spent her time in the barn and corrals, nurturing her need to be important to someone or something.

The horses didn't judge her and they always welcomed her. She learned everything she could from anyone who would teach her. Then she found out more simply by spending all her time with the equines. Although they couldn't speak, they did tell her what she needed to know to train them.

It was as though she'd found a new family to accept her.

Her brothers and sisters respected her work with the animals, but that didn't mean they stopped bothering her about everything else. How she dressed, how she acted, how often she bathed, or if she brushed her hair. No matter how much she tried to live her life by her own rules, the Grahams kept telling her how and what to do.

Matt was the worst of the lot, although even Rebecca could be unintentionally cruel with her comments. No one made much of an effort to accept her way of doing things. They simply tolerated her, which hurt more than telling her she needed to comb her hair.

Ben had pulled farther and farther away until he was a familiar stranger who disappeared for weeks, sometimes a month at a time. Rebecca had moved to town and Cat was once more alone in a crowd.

When she met James, he didn't judge her, nor did he try to change her, even if he didn't approve. She was fascinated by the handsome, dark-haired man, even after she discovered he was a

Gibson. He had an annoying habit of blurting out whatever was on his mind, but he'd never treated her as if she was less than he was, except for once at the wedding, when he told her to stick to female work, but even then she'd known he was simply trying to keep his distance.

It was unusual. Refreshing. Addictive.

The more she was around him, the more she found herself becoming attached to him. The only problem was, he avoided her most of the time, which made her more anxious to be with him.

Now here they were alone. And she'd fulfilled the fantasy of being with a man. Cock to pussy. Something she'd wondered about since her sisters had told her what happened between men and women. James was the only man she'd ever wanted to be with. He didn't appear to be falling to his knees and pledging his love, however.

Cat wasn't sure how she felt about that. Did she love him? Or was she in love with the idea of a man who saw her for who she was? For the first time in a long time, she wished her sisters and sisters-in-law were there. She needed to talk to someone about what she was doing. Or not doing.

Although she'd done plenty already.

She should be thinking about the horses, not the man beside her. The idea someone was mistreating her beloved animals made her stomach hurt enough she thought she'd puke. James distracted her from the panic taking hold.

"You're too quiet. I'm suspicious."

She didn't expect to laugh at his very serious observation, but she did. "I was thinking."

"Even more suspicious."

She reached over and punched him in the arm.

"Ow! Damn, woman, do you have iron hands?" He rubbed at his bicep. "What do they feed you at that ranch?"

She showed him a closed fist and shook it at him. "Don't insult me and I won't bring my hammer."

"Those thieves should be shaking in their boots."

"Damn straight."

"I suspect your brothers and Aurora taught you how to swing that particular hammer."

She shrugged, her amusement gone. "What makes you think I

needed someone to teach me?"

"You're prickly." He shook his head. "No matter what I say, it lands on the wrong side of your mood."

She opened her mouth to tell him he was rude, but closed it. The truth, which was hard to swallow, was that she *was* prickly. It was the way she dealt with people when she got her back up. Eva used to tell her she turned into a hedgehog when she wanted to hide and a porcupine when she was threatened.

Prickly was an apt description, much as she'd like to deny it.

"Be careful, then. You don't want to be on my bad side," she said primly.

He snorted. "I don't need that warning. I learned it last year."

"Sometimes people aren't what they seem." She hadn't intended on saying that to him, but the words escaped her mouth before she could catch them.

"Truth." His tone had changed, become softer.

"I reckon you aren't what you seem either."

He shook his head. "And I reckon no one is what they seem like. We all wear a mask for everyone else to see. Nobody likes being judged."

She couldn't help but be curious after that particular piece of knowledge. "Who judges you? The Gibsons don't take shit from anyone, no matter what. I heard that. I've seen that."

He was silent for a few minutes. "I've been judged since the day I was born. My mother didn't really know who my father was and she sure as hell didn't want me. Or Tobias. Or Will."

She didn't reply. Shock held her tongue. Cat had no idea the Gibsons' mother had bastard children, ones she didn't want or love. Rebecca hadn't revealed any of that information. Knowing her sister, it was probably because she didn't feel it was her place to share it. Cat knew James's grandfather had been raising them, but nothing about his parents. At the core of Cat's life was a family who loved her. She'd lost her parents when she was a little girl, but she still remembered her mother's love. The sweet smell of her mother's scented soap and how it enveloped Cat when she hugged her mama.

"Did I judge you?" she asked, hoping he would say no.

"No. That's one reason I like you, Catherine. You don't give shit, but you don't take it either." He smiled at her and damned if her traitorous heart didn't do a little jig. When he wanted to be, James was a natural charmer.

"I still don't like you," she lied, lied, lied. For the first time in her life, she wanted a man to want to be with her. Not because he had to. Because he wanted to.

He shrugged. "In my experience, folks don't have to like each other to respect each other."

"I expect that's true." She respected few people and most of them were family or had married into her family. James had done some bad things in his life, but he'd grown up since then. So had she.

"You should do what you want and to hell with what everyone else thinks. Be Cat or be Catherine. You should be the one to decide." With that pronouncement, he knocked the breath from her body.

It took a few minutes for her to put a thought together. James was a man who made her question everything she held to be true. Including her opinion of herself. "I lied. I do like you."

He turned and met her gaze. "Good. Real good."

CHAPTER SEVEN

They followed the tracks, still staying at least four hours behind the herd, if not more. Frustration made her want to scream at the sky. Determination made her keep pushing forward until she nearly fell out of the saddle.

"I need to stop."

"Damn right." James shook his head. "Should have stopped an hour ago. I gotta piss like a race horse."

Cat laughed, her voice husky from pure exhaustion. "Glad I'm not offended easy."

He pulled his gelding to a stop and dismounted with natural grace. She pulled Paladin to a stop and blew out a breath. She was sore and stiff, confused and in need of some sleep.

This time they'd found a small creek with soft, sweet grass and the gentle sound of the wind in the leaves.

It looked like paradise to her.

"C'mon down from there, Catherine." He held out his hands to help her down.

She stared at him, shocked and touched by the offer. It had been at least ten years, if not more, since someone had thought to assist her in dismounting. Never mind that she didn't need any help.

"You surprise me."

He tipped his hat. "You surprise me too."

His large hands wrapped around her middle and she closed her eyes, enjoying the sensation and the strength in his touch. She could get used to it.

When her feet touched the ground, he didn't step away. He didn't remove his hands. She hadn't stood so close to him before.

He was at least eight inches taller than her. Her head skimmed the bottom of his chin.

She put her hand in the center of his chest. The steady thump of his heart pressed against her palm. His body heat surrounded her. Her body warmed, and a now-familiar ache began between her legs. Her pussy might not have had more than one encounter, but it knew what it wanted.

James Gibson.

"I need—"

He abruptly stepped back and she swayed toward him. "Let's get the horses unsaddled and let them drink up. Then we can fill our canteens and wash."

She stared at him, her mouth open as he turned his back on her. She hadn't imagined that connection, that moment. James chose to ignore it.

Disgruntled to be needy but unfulfilled, Cat turned her attention to her mount. After taking care of his needs, she retrieved clean clothes from her saddle bag and returned to the creek. Her annoying companion could build a fire and set up camp. She was going to wash off the grime and rinse out the clothes she was wearing.

Cat told herself not to expect too much from James. They'd made no promises to each other. Their partnership was temporary, as apparently was their physical relationship.

She undressed and stepped into the waist-high water. A yelp of pure discomfort leapt from her mouth.

"Holy shit!"

James was there in an instant, pistol in one hand, rifle in the other. Ready to do battle. For her. Just when she was ready to dismiss him for being his usual jackass, he redeemed himself.

"What's wrong?"

"The water is cold as a well digger's ass." She shivered and wondered if this was the perfect way to cure her need to have sex with James.

"Jesus Christ on crackers, woman." He shoved the pistol into its holster. "You scared the hell out of me."

She blinked, forgetting about her lower half growing numb. "You were worried about me."

"A'course I was. You're my responsibility."

Now she frowned. "That's the only reason."

His gaze slid down to her chest. To her extremely hard nipples that seemed to grow impossibly achy. "You're, ah, cold."

"That's what I said."

"Why are you naked?"

She held up the bar of soap in her hand. "I'm washing up."

He looked down at the ground in front him. "I could use a good washing too."

Her heart slammed into her ribs. Exhaustion gone. "Then shuck your clothes and join me."

He reached for the buttons on his shirt and pulled the garment off. His chest was magnificently formed. Dark whorls of hair covered slabs of muscle and flesh. He had a few scars, white against the honeyed color of his skin.

Sweet heavenly saints, she wanted to explore.

The night before, she had seen nothing under the blanket. This was like a feast for her eyes and she couldn't wait to see what was beneath his trousers.

He set his shirt on a nearby branch and stopped dead. His arm extended, his expression hard as stone.

"What—"

"Shh," he cut her off.

She could have argued with him, but life on a Texas ranch taught her to be cautious when someone scented danger. His hand slid to the pistol still on his hip. She wished like hell she wasn't naked, vulnerable and useless. She hadn't considered the possibility of being hurt or worse. No, Cat had done what she usually did—whatever she wanted to.

Stealthy as a fish, she slid close to the embankment where he crept forward, pistol drawn. Cat grabbed her own weapon and went after him. That's when she heard it.

A whimper. A small cry of an animal. Her gut clenched with fear and all her body's needs flew away on the wind. She listened hard, willing away all the distractions.

She heard it again and tapped James on the back. He turned to scowl at her, and then his eyes widened as his gaze slid down to her naked tits. She'd forgotten she wasn't clothed, but it didn't matter. She pointed to the left.

He shook his head but followed her direction and they both

moved forward, silent on the leaf-covered ground. Their own mounts grew restless, whinnying from their position on the other side of the trees.

Cat sniffed the air. Blood. There was no mistaking it. She pushed past James and got to her feet, jumping over the row of bushes. There on the ground, abandoned and still covered in blood was a foal.

She didn't remember screaming but she fell to her knees and picked up the tiny body. It was too early, far too early for the baby to be born. The stress from being taken must have forced the mare to early delivery.

"Oh, baby, I'm so sorry."

The foal was alive, but barely. He had obviously not stood, nor been nursed. An early birth meant a quick death. Instead of caring for the animal, the bastards had left him to die, alone and cold.

Tears stung her eyes for the cruelty and the loss. She cupped his small head and spotted the white blaze between his ears. This was Starling's foal, the beautiful mare who had been a mother for the first time.

The thieves had stolen more than the horses. They'd stolen a baby from its mother, a life from the hope of the future. Grief clogged her throat as she held his quivering body.

"Catherine." James wrapped his shirt around the foal. "I'm so sorry."

Cat wasn't the type of female who cried at the least provocation. She couldn't remember the last time she'd shed true tears. Now was the time for an exception. James snuggled up behind her and held them both, his arms warm and welcome. She let the tears fall as she rocked the small miracle that had been denied a chance, holding him so he wouldn't die alone.

They buried the foal in a patch of sunshine by the bank of the creek. Cat had stopped crying but she remained silent. He'd never seen her express such emotion. He wanted to comfort her but he didn't know how. All he did was hold her while she'd cried for the poor creature even after the tears ceased.

If he knew anything about Cat, she would put aside her grief quickly and let her anger take over. Now that the thieves had cost the life of one of the expected foals, she would unleash an unequaled fury on the faceless men.

Cat quiet was more frightening than when she shouted. He stirred the fire and retrieved the pot of coffee from the corner of the blaze. As he poured two cups, he watched Cat as she ran her knife on the sharpening stone she'd pulled from her saddlebags.

"You have a task in mind for that blade?"

She grunted. "If we're lucky."

The memory of holding a naked, weeping Cat would stay with him for a long time. She was the strongest woman he knew. He hadn't realized the depth of love she had for the horses she raised and trained. She'd insisted on putting up a small cross by the horse's grave.

That was love. It shouldn't surprise him she could become so involved with the animals. The Grahams seemed to have perfected the right way to love. Cat might not show it, but she felt it nonetheless.

"I'm going to kill them."

James wasn't surprised to hear it but he didn't think she meant it.

"Then you'd hang for their murders."

"It would be worth it." She narrowed her gaze. "Fucking sons of bitches killed that foal and might kill his mother if she's not taken care of properly."

He hadn't mentioned the potential condition of the mare. She might be the next carcass they found. If he was right, Cat would search to the end of the earth to find the horses and the men who took them. Their task had rolled from chasing the horses to hunting the men.

James knew he wouldn't stop her but he had to stay with her and keep her as safe as he could. Possibly keep her from a noose if she attempted murder.

"We need to get up before the sun. Given how long the, ah, foal was lying there, they may have been here two hours before we got here." She slid the knife into the scabbard in her boot. "I plan to find them before they can kill another one of my horses."

"Your brother was a Texas Ranger." He had to try to talk to sense into her.

"That has nothing to do with this."

"It has everything to do with it. You know he'd tell you to let the law take care of them."

She threw her arms wide, her blue eyes snapping sparks. "There ain't no law out here, Gibson. It's only survival and who draws their gun faster. I plan on winning."

"You could get yourself killed."

She shrugged. "I'll take a few of them with me. I expect you'll finish them off."

He couldn't reason with her. "You've lost your mind, woman."

"It is what it is."

"Why are you so hell bent on vengeance? This is exactly what almost destroyed Tobias." James didn't know how he felt about Cat, but he didn't want her to commit murder, be killed, or hanged. She was unique and he wanted to keep her at his side. Possibly forever.

"It's not vengeance, it's justice."

He snorted. "That's what vigilantes say."

"I'm not a vigilante. I'm protecting what's mine."

"That's what Tobias said before we followed the tracks that led us to the Circle Eight." James suffered from tremendous guilt for his part in burning down the ranch house and barn. No matter that he'd been fifteen or that his older brother had ordered him to do it. James had a choice and he'd chosen badly. "That didn't turn out so well, did it?"

"Shut up, James." She pointed at him. "There's a world of difference between what you did and what I'm gonna do."

"How? Tobias was protecting his family. Vaughn had stolen money and a deed from Pops. My grandfather was an old man and was taken advantage of." James had to get her to see the truth. "Tobias thought what he'd done was the right thing to do because he was blinded by anger and hurt."

She opened her mouth to say something equally as contentious and he held up his hand.

"We ain't gonna see eye to eye on this but I want you think about what I said. There's damn little difference between vengeance and justice."

She rolled her eyes. "As long as you shut up about it, then I'll agree to think about it."

James wanted to say more, but he understood she wasn't going to listen to him. Not then. It was up to him to keep her safe, no matter what.

There was no other choice.

Cat woke when the sky was dark gray, just as night was giving way to the dawn. James was already awake, poking at the fire with a stick, his expression in shadows. Sleeping beside him had been different the second night. There had been no arousal, no sweet surrender to her urges.

Instead, she needed his comfort, much to her chagrin. Her grief was still sharp, but not as devastating as it had been the day before. She would still seek justice for the crimes committed against the Circle Eight and her horses.

What she didn't know was what James would do to stop her. Was he stubborn enough to get in the way of her gun if she took aim? He seemed intent on convincing her to stop seeking that which she was due. As if a Gibson had any idea how to find justice. She wasn't going to be committing a crime. She would be protecting what was hers and making sure they understood not to ever steal from the Grahams again.

She washed up at the creek and started packing her gear. James was already done saddling his gelding and was just about to saddle Paladin. To her surprise, the horse let him do it.

The gelding was a bit of a snob and didn't allow many people to tend to him. She normally trusted people that her horse took to. It wasn't as if she didn't like James, but at the moment, she wasn't feeling too charitable toward him.

Losing the foal had been like a punch to the gut. She was sore and sad, angry and frustrated. James was a convenient excuse to express those feelings. He thought he was trying to make her see logic, but he was really just making her that much more intent on killing the men who hurt her.

"I wasn't the type of girl to let anyone hurt me without hurting them back." She spoke as she swung the saddlebags up on Paladin. "I guess I never outgrew it."

He plopped his hat on his head and looked at her with his dark eyes. "I never let anyone get close enough to hurt me."

The connection between them shimmered on the air, growing

stronger. She had considered him handsome and was interested in him, but there was much more. He was more like her than she expected.

"We should get moving." He handed her Paladin's reins. "I've got jerky we can gnaw on as we ride."

"I want to check the tracks to make sure we get on the right trail." Cat didn't want to make a single mistake, but at the same time, she had an urgent need to ride as hard as she could.

"Already did. They're still heading north." He hesitated.

"And what else? Don't you dare hold back on me, Gibson." She had to make him see that if they were going to be partners, they had to trust each other.

"There's a blood trail, it's faint but I saw it."

She clenched her teeth against the cry of pain. "Starling."

"Likely. A mare that foals early is likely to bleed more after. She needs care and they ain't stopping for nothing." He pointed at the eastern horizon. "If we ride hard we can catch them."

Her throat grew tight. "Yep."

After spending two full days and two nights with James, she had come to know his many expressions. Sometimes there were subtle differences, but after studying the man, she saw them. Understood them.

Was that what it meant to be close to someone? Her sisters and brothers had been a part of her life for too long. She didn't have to think about how to behave with them. James was new but familiar at the same time.

They rode side by side, watching for tracks, always scanning before, after, to the right and left. It was a comfortable silence between them. They had a shared purpose. A refreshing change for Cat. She was usually at odds with everyone she worked with.

Not so with the man who made her want to shoot him. Now she felt different. More like herself rather than who other people wanted her to be. She could hardly believe it was James who unknowingly provided her the freedom.

Cat was distracted by her thoughts about the man who rode beside her. When she finally realized what was there in front of her, it was too late.

The horses, the thieves and loaded weapons.

CHAPTER EIGHT

James reached for his pistol when Cat reacted. Badly.

"Fucking hell!" Her voice carried across the meadow they'd stumbled into. He'd heard her brother Matt use that particular curse before. Cat obviously picked it up for her own use.

The four men were sitting on the various logs and rocks with the horses behind them tied to a lead line. The yearlings kicked and whinnied, not caring who was on the receiving end of their hooves. The mares pushed the foals to the edges of the line, away from danger.

The largest of the men got to his feet. He was built like an oak tree with massive arms and chest, but bowlegged. His hair was black as soot beneath a well-worn hat, clothes dirty enough to walk on their own, and a stare that might set rocks on fire.

"Who the hell are you?" His voice was as sharp as the knife strapped to his right thigh.

Cat's eyes narrowed. "Who the hell are you?"

"God damn, you're a female." The big man snorted. "Ain't you never heard a woman don't wear trousers?"

"My woman doesn't like dresses." James gestured to her. "She's a fair hand with the beeves and horses, and britches are best for that."

His heart resided somewhere in his throat, but he kept his expression and his voice even and calm. If Cat managed to keep her wits, they might survive the next few minutes. He'd been distracted by thoughts of her and he hadn't noticed that they'd stumbled onto their quarry until it was too late. Now they could die in an instant.

And he hadn't told her he was falling in love with her.

That she made him feel alive, needed, worthy.

Now he might never get the chance to tell her any of it.

"She cusses like a man too. You sure she ain't got a dick?" The stranger taunted them, but James didn't even blink. Cat pulled her pistol from its holster, the barrel pointed at the ground.

"I don't care one fucking bit if your men cut me down. I'll kill you before they blink if you insult me again." She cocked the pistol so fast, her hand was a blur.

James wasn't the only one surprised. The rest of the men moved backward, away from the danger of the woman who had bigger balls than all of them. The leader crossed his arms, making his chest appear larger. His action told James that the man wasn't threatened by Cat.

It would make her livid.

To his surprise, she only tightened her grip on the pistol. James was proud of her and pleased to know she was as intelligent as he suspected. They didn't sneak up on the thieves, they stumbled across them, and now their lives hung in the balance.

"I like her," the big man pronounced. He turned his dark gaze to James. "Now tell me what the fuck you're doing here."

James met Cat's gaze. He saw the desperation and fear, but he also saw the determination and anger. The woman had grit.

"Looking for work." James kept his tone guarded.

"What kind of work do you do?" The stranger eyed Cat's figure before he glanced at James.

"Whatever needs doing."

The other man nodded. "I got a few of those on my crew."

"You need two more?" James didn't let Cat speak to his crazy question. "We ain't got nowhere to be anytime soon and we could use the money."

The man spit a brown stream of tobacco juice at the ground. "We gotta job that only needs four men."

"I can kill two of them, then you'd need us." Cat gestured with her free hand. "Pick the two who ain't pulling their weight."

There was some nervous laughter from the rest of the men. None of them probably knew whether or not she meant it. James thought maybe she did.

"Funny girl. I might could need someone to ride point. We

maybe got someone on our tail so we gotta move fast." The stranger gestured to the yearlings that were still kicking up a storm. "These little fucking shits won't listen to a one of us. Somebody ain't done their job training 'em right."

Cat looked at the horses then shrugged. "I have a bit of experience with young ones."

The man's gaze narrowed. "Show me."

She dismounted with her usual grace and the men nodded. Whether in appreciation or surprise, he couldn't say. She tucked the pistol in its holster and took a leather strop from her saddlebag.

James had a feeling whatever she was going to do would hurt her worse than it would the horses. She stepped close to one to the fractious horses, yanked on his bit and laid the strap across his neck. The horse's whinny turned to more of a scream. She yanked again and whispered in its ear. The quivering yearling pressed against her shoulder. After a few more seconds, its head dropped and she stepped away.

When she turned to look at the men, she kept hold of the horse's bit. Her expression was carved from stone. "That good enough?"

"Damn, she's tough." The big man nodded. "You two can stay. I'll give you two dollars a day. One for her."

James took a moment, as though he was contemplating the offer. He could see Cat was nearly vibrating with rage, but she held her tongue. He didn't expect to find himself admiring her, but he did far more than that. He fell more in love with her more every moment. Since now was not a particularly good time to acknowledge his feelings, he kept hold of them with iron will, lest something show on his face. He could have laughed at the stupidity of his heart.

"Two for her, three for me." James gestured to hr. "If she can tame the lot of them, and I ride point, we can move real fast."

"I'm Chino. This here's Red, Al and Whitey." The other men nodded as they were introduced.

James didn't hesitate, knowing the man could probably smell a lie. "Jeb and Katie." Close enough they would answer to the names, but nothing to tie them to the Circle Eight or the Grahams. His feckless mother taught him if he was going to tell a lie to make it as close to reality as he could make it. A half-truth, a murky lie.

"Make yourself useful then. Them horses ain't gonna mind unless somebody makes 'em." With that Chino turned away.

James wondered if he'd just sentenced he and Cat to death.

Bile crept up the back of her throat, almost choking her. She'd used violence and a lie so big it hurt her heart. The yearling, called Biscuit because of his light coloring, eyed her with fear. She held the tears back through force of will. She could not, would not, cry in front of Chino and his cohorts.

James had saved himself and Cat with his quick thinking. She'd wanted to shoot them dead on sight. However, both of them would have died and possibly the horses, then the thieves would get away with their crime. Even now her hand itched to pull out the pistol and shoot them.

If they were as dumb as she expected, they wouldn't notice the brand on Paladin matched the ones on the mares. The yearling hadn't yet been branded since most would be sold. She longed to check each and every horse, but she had to maintain a cool detachment.

She staked Paladin away from the other animals. There was no need for more shenanigans from any of them. She had a trick she used on the young ones by flicking their ears. However if she'd done that in front of the gang, they might have suspected her. Cat's methods were unique amongst horse trainers and any familiarity she had with the horses would be revealed if they obeyed straight away.

Instead she had to hurt Biscuit using techniques she had refused to use. Ever. Hurting him had scraped across her conscience and her heart. It would be some time before he trusted her, but he would fear her.

Not what she wanted but she would swallow her disgust and do what had to be done. Cat was always telling her brothers to trust her, to let her use her own methods to work. She complained about not being trusted or respected. Now she had to rely on herself and James to save themselves and the herd, no matter what she had to do.

She would find her inner strength and the way to bring

everyone home. It didn't matter if she was scared or away from home. Far from home.

She couldn't be afraid.

Cat finished settling the younger horses. Biscuit shied away from her but he did as he was bade. The mares crowded her and she would swear Starling wept on Cat's shoulder.

Maintaining her expression became more difficult with each passing moment. She checked each mare, pleased to see that they were all in relatively good shape. Except Starling. The mare was raw and had flies in and around her vagina. From what Cat could tell, she had never delivered the placenta and her teats were swollen with unexpressed milk. Infection would most certainly set in.

Starling would die. There was no way for Cat to save her now. Not without proper medical help, and perhaps not even then.

Cat's heart cracked as she took care of the horse as best she could. She filled her mind with ways to make the men pay for what they'd done to her beautiful animal. Starling appeared confused and begging for help. Cat could only do small things. It was too late to do any more.

"That one popped out a foal on us." Chino spoke from behind her. The man's gravelly voice made Cat jump.

"She's not going to make it much farther." Cat kept her voice as dead as she wanted the man to be.

"That's money out of my pocket."

Cat turned to look at him, her palm itching to shoot the son of a bitch between the eyes. "Then somebody should have taken care of her after she gave birth. Her teats are swollen and the placenta is still inside her. Flies are eating her alive. That ain't how you take care of a horse."

Chino's dark brows went up. "You got a mouth on you, woman."

"The name is Katie and I'm telling you like it is." She turned back to Starling to hide her rage. The man had no idea what he'd done.

He touched Cat's arm and she jumped away, pistol in hand in seconds. Chino grinned, his tobacco-stained teeth on display.

"I'm betting you're a wildcat in bed."

She cocked the pistol. "Too bad you'll never find out. Don't ever touch me again or I'll blow your fucking balls off."

"Everything all right over here?" James appeared on her right. He stared at Chino, his hand on his own pistol. The air grew thick with tension.

"Your woman talks too much." Chino narrowed his gaze but Cat didn't lower her weapon.

"She has a tendency to do that. Big mouth but she's mine." James put his hand on her shoulder.

"If the mare is going to die, then get rid of her now. I ain't gonna pay you to take care of a dying horse." Chino turned and left as abruptly as he came, leaving more death in his wake.

"I'm going to kill him." Her voice erupted in a low growl. The men were all within ten feet of her, so close, so dangerous.

James leaned to whisper in her ear. "Not yet. Now we gotta figure out their weak points and take care of the horses so they survive."

"He wants me to put Starling down." The words cracked just like her heart.

"It's the humane thing to do. She's not gonna survive, even if we get her back to the Circle Eight." James was too damn logical.

"I hate you."

"You've told me that before."

"I mean it."

"I know you do." He kissed her temple. "Be strong."

She blinked away stinging in her eyes. Damn emotions got in the way sometimes. She didn't want to put Starling down, but the men were right. It would be cruel to keep the horse in the state she was in. The flies could have done more damage inside her, causing her agony.

"Do you want me to do it?"

She shook her head. "I'll do it. I'm going to use a knife to keep the noise to a minimum. No need to call attention to this band of miscreants and put the rest of the animals and us in danger."

She pulled the knife from her boot and took Starling's lead rope. As she walked a distance away, James followed, his steps as heavy as hers. The mare's head drooped low and her gait was wobbly. Cat could barely make her feet move, but she dug deep for the strength to do what needed to be done.

A large cottonwood tree hung over a patch of sweet grass. Starling nibbled on the treat while Cat prepared herself to take the life of the horse she had brought into the world.

Grief threatened to overwhelm her. She bit the inside of her cheek and the pain snapped her back. "C'mon, girl, lay down for me."

Seemingly exhausted, the horse lowered herself to the ground. Cat knelt beside her, stroking the mare's neck. Her chest ached hard enough to steal her breath.

James stood guard, watching over her, shielding her from the men who were close enough to see them but not near enough to hear them. This was a private moment that had to be public. Resentment, anger and sadness swirled in her gut as she positioned the knife against the horse's throat.

"I'm sorry, my beautiful girl." She slit fast and deep, hitting the artery. Starling jerked at the pain from the knife, but then she let out a long breath, perhaps in relief. Cat bit her cheek so hard, she drew blood, just as the mare's lifeblood spilled into the rich green grass.

"Oh God, James." She couldn't help the sob that escaped.

"Be strong, Catherine," he repeated. "We will save the rest of them or kill these bastards for what they did." The fierceness in his tone helped her gain control of herself.

As the life drained from Starling's body, Cat soothed the mare, showing her love and affection. The unfairness of the loss of the horse and her foal made the fury bubble up again. She had to remain calm and keep the rest of the herd alive.

Cat was very afraid she wouldn't be able to do that. And possibly cost James and her lives in the name of vengeance.

CHAPTER NINE

They moved north as a group with everyone working to keep the horses in check. Everyone took a few lead ropes and Cat had the foals and mares in her control. Chino sent James ahead to scout their route, looking for water and potential spots for nasty surprises. It was almost a normal day.

Except for the fact these four men had stolen about two dozen horses and through their actions, killed a mare and her foal.

Life hadn't been normal for James, now or ever. He'd dealt with bad people in his life from the time he could remember being with his mother. She had a tendency to pick the men who would treat her the worst. That meant they treated him like a stray dog that needed to be kicked.

He'd been kicked more times than he'd ever been held or kissed in his life. Cat was the first person in his life who accepted him for who he was. Even Tobias had trouble finding a way to be his brother. Will had been the closest thing he had to a friend, even as a brother. Unfortunately, he was now a boy trapped in the body of a grown man.

James had to protect himself all his life. Today was no different, and yet it was. Today he had Cat to protect as well. She was important to him, as much as she drove him crazy. The woman had little sense of self-preservation and balls of steel.

And damned if he wasn't in love with her. Hell, he'd been half in love with her six months earlier when he first visited the Circle Eight. She'd followed him around and made him notice her. Showed him what he'd been missing by shutting himself off from everyone and everything.

Now they were tied together. There was no going back.

The day was long and dusty. There hadn't been much rain in the last week so the group of horses kicked up quite a bit of the Texas dirt. James was lucky to be ahead of the group rather than riding drag with Cat. But she hadn't complained about her position in their group.

If he were honest with himself, he was more worried about her tangling with Chino again. The big man watched her with sharp eyes and an intelligence the other three men lacked.

The horses kept with her. She used her skills and taught Whitey, Red and Al how to hold the leads for the herd to keep everyone at a reasonable pace. The foals were the most at risk but Cat had control of the speed at which they moved.

"Where your people from?" Chino rode up beside James.

"Here and there." James wasn't lying about that. "My mama had a pair of wandering feet."

"My pa did too." Chino spat a stream of tobacco juice toward the ground. "Spent plenty of time not knowing where my next meal came from."

"My belly scratched at my back more days than not." James shrugged. "I found a way to get what I needed."

A hawk cried from above, gliding on the wind. Its shadow passed over the bigger man.

"What put you in my path?" Chino's casual question was anything but casual.

"Coincidence. We finished up a job at a ranch down south. Round-ups are going on so we move around getting work where we can." James kept with the partial truth again.

"I don't believe in coincidences." Chino gestured with his head. "The woman is crazy."

"She's damn good with horses and beeves though. Works harder than most men." Another true statement.

"Why the hell does she wear trousers?"

James laughed. "I don't know. Probably because she's crazy."

"But she's your woman?"

"She shares my bedroll every night." At least she had for the last two days.

"I'm guessing she hides hits tits under that getup?" Chino was now baiting him, but James wasn't going to react.

"She's a woman. They all got the same equipment." James

pointed at a cloud of dust in the distance. "Is that riders?"

Chino was momentarily distracted. "Whitey, give Al your lead ropes and ride on over there."

The cowboy galloped off toward what was probably just a dust devil. James didn't know how long he and Cat could pretend to be wandering souls. Chino was already suspicious. No doubt he had some kind of test planned to flush out the truth. They couldn't afford for that to happen.

Tonight they would need to formulate a plan because the farce couldn't continue. The horses weren't in good shape and some were downright raggedy. There wasn't enough water or grass to feed this many horses. Why would someone want to steal horses only to damage them before selling them?

It made no sense and that bothered James. A lot. He understood about thieving to survive, but this crime wasn't that. This was more like a specific snatch to hurt the Grahams or the Circle Eight.

It was personal.

Whitey returned to report a whole lot of nothing. They moved on the rest of the day, resting briefly for water. The men had no feed for the herd and relied on the availability of grass. No wonder the horses were beginning to lose weight. They'd not been groomed in days, even after riding hard.

It was a wonder that Cat kept all her rage inside. James wondered how long she'd be able to keep it contained.

Cat knew it was a matter of time before Chino made his way to her side. He'd been watching her since they started riding together. She kept her attention on the horses, but her instincts told her to always keep the big man in front of her.

He'd been riding with James for hours. After the last stop, Chino rode beside her. The foals scampered away from him and she had a time getting them back under control.

She glared at Chino. "You're paying me to move these horses. Getting them riled up isn't helping."

"I ain't paid you yet. Keep 'em on their leashes or I'll leave them behind." He didn't appear to care about the babies. Any fool knew healthy foals were the future of any herd.

"You're driving them hard. The little ones aren't going to be able to go on much longer." She gestured to the dirty, matted hair. "They could use a curry brush too."

"I ain't being paid to groom these fucking horses."

Cat kept her expression neutral but she wanted to scream at him for his neglect. She had to find out information before she and James killed these bastards. Starling and her foal would not have died in vain.

"Somebody isn't going to pay you much for them if they're dead."

Chino didn't respond for a few moments. "I'll do what needs doing with the buyer. I took what I was hired to. It ain't my fault if they die."

"Huh, so the horses are stolen." Cat gestured to the foals. "These babies aren't going to fetch much."

"Eh, like I said, I did what needed doing. That family is high and mighty, pissing on everyone else like kings." Chino grunted. "Fucking sons of bitches won't be so cocky no more."

"I don't like cocky people. Think they can tell me how to dress, how to act." She snorted. "I am what I want to be, not what they want me to be."

"I think you're crazy."

"You wouldn't be the first."

"Your man lets you run wild."

"Jeb doesn't *let* me do anything."

"I expect that's true."

"Who are these cocky people you hate?" She needed him to tell her why. Dammit.

"Ain't no difference, is it?"

"I suppose not." She looked at the horses. "They got a lot of horses though."

"They got everything and people like me got nothing. It ain't right, I tell ya." Chino seemed to hate the Grahams as if they'd wronged him personally. She'd never seen or heard of him. Who the hell was his boss?

"Your boss doesn't like them either, huh?"

"I ain't got a boss. People pay me for a job, that's all."

"Hopefully me and Jeb can avoid them." She didn't ask for the name. She just let it hang in the air. It was up to Chino to respond.

"They got these unnatural eyes, ain't blue and ain't green." He snapped his gaze to hers. "What color your eyes, girlie?"

Cat widened her eyes. "Blue. I've never seen eyes both blue and green. That is unnatural."

That's my family, you rat bastard.

"Now you know to steer clear of 'em."

I'm gonna steer my way clear to shoot you.

"Much obliged for telling me."

They continued on in silence for a while. Cat wanted to ask him the question foremost on her mind, but she didn't want to spook him. She had to know who hated the Grahams enough to steel their yearlings, breeding stock and foals. Someone who resented them with enough edge to try to destroy them.

She kept the conversation neutral, much as she didn't want to. "How many days you gonna need us?"

"One more day. We get where we're going by sundown tomorrow."

"That's an easy 'nother two dollars for me." She wiped her nose on her sleeve. "Got any other work from this rich person who doesn't care how many horses you deliver?"

"Why?" His voice had sharpened.

"Those dollars won't last long. We gotta eat." She glanced at him, noting his guarded expression. "If you don't have anything, then that's the end of it. Me and Jeb like to keep on the move."

Chino must've heard what he wanted to hear because he moved away to yell at Whitey for something he'd done wrong. Cat breathed an inner sigh of relief to be out of his line of sight.

She and James had to come up with a plan for the next twelve hours or they might not live to see another sunrise. Time was ticking hard and fast in her ear. They had to triumph. Grahams didn't know how to give up.

Cat would get her horses or die trying.

Ben had wondered if he would ever find the right trail. Then after he picked that up, he wondered if he would find his sister. They moved fast and long. He was exhausted by the end of the first day.

The second day he rose before the sun but Cat had at least a twelve-hour start on him and he'd had to double back a few times before he hit on the right set of tracks.

It was near dark when he found the horse's body. The twilight had turned everything into a steel-gray color so the carcass was no more than a lump against the horizon.

He dismounted and approached the object. His stomach fell to his feet when he recognized the brand on the animal's rump. That was a Circle Eight horse, which meant one of Cat's herd was gone.

The flies buzzed around him, excited by the kill. The smell of blood greeted him as he grew closer. The coppery scent was rancid in the waning heat of the day. He squatted down and peered at the horse's coloring.

"Fuck." He would recognize Starling anywhere. She was Cat's favorite mare. When she was a filly, the damn thing followed Cat around like a puppy.

The mare's throat had been cut at the artery. A deliberate kill. He looked her over and noted the flies concentrated around her hind end. The mare had lost her foal somewhere and must've been dying from the trauma.

He would bet it had been Cat that put Starling down. The cut was too precise and exact. Someone wanted the death to be quick. Horse thieves would have left the animal to die alone.

Ben got to his feet and looked around. The horse had been dead maybe eight hours. He was catching up to them. If he rode another few hours before stopping, he would overtake them in the morning at some point.

He swung back up into the saddle and patted his horse's neck. "Let's find them, boy."

They stopped riding just as dark overtook the day's dying light. James had scouted the spot to camp. There was a creek nearby and some trees for shelter and to secure the horses. It wasn't perfect, but they had what they needed.

James was exhausted from maintaining the façade of Jeb again. Damned if he didn't feel himself creeping back into that skin after having shed it years ago. Jeb was a different person than James. He was dark, cynical and had little hope for the future.

James was mature enough to hope for a future with Cat. If

they survived the next day, it was possible. He wouldn't make any plans, but the potential for something extraordinary flickered in his heart.

As he dismounted and drank deep from the canteen to chase away the heat of the day, he knew he'd been lucky enough not to be riding drag. Cat, however, was not so lucky. She had a fine coating of dust on her skin and clothes. As he watched, she took off her hat and slapped it against her leg. A cloud of dirt rose up around her.

She didn't complain. She simply swiped her face with her neckerchief and slapped the hat back on. James had never pictured himself with a wife. He could now, however, imagine Cat beside him. An equal partner.

Damn.

He had to stop focusing on what could be and think about how to survive. He knew how to switch his mind but he had no idea how to switch his heart. If anything happened to Cat, he'd never forgive himself.

"Get them young'uns tied up and watered," Chino spoke aloud as though everyone was on duty, which James supposed they all were. "Run a line between the trees to secure the rest of 'em."

Chino sat on a rock and rolled a cigarette, watching everyone as they moved around the camp. Horses were unsaddled, watered, secured, firewood retrieved and a blaze started. Cat and James didn't even know these men and yet they all did what was necessary.

What they didn't have was rhythm. Work got done, but people bumped into each other, toes were squashed, curses were thrown. It was a chaotic mess with Chino lording over all of it. The difference between what he'd experienced on the Circle Eight and this sorry band of misfits was astonishing.

The Grahams and their ranch hands moved with harmony, respect and purpose. This experience with the thieves was the exact opposite. Discord, rancor and resentment hung in the air.

James took care of the mares along with his gelding and Paladin. Cat sent him a grateful glance as she wrangled the yearlings. Most of them listened to her, but the light-colored one shied away from her touch. She'd used a whip on him and there was no doubt in James's mind that the moment would always stand between horse and woman.

It took much longer to get all their tasks done because no one listened to anyone else. A full hour after they'd stopped for the night, the fire was going, coffee was on and the men were huddled around the blaze. James watched them as Cat went to the creek to wash up.

He waited at least ten minutes before he gave into the impulse to follow her. The gray light of twilight had given way to the blue shade of night. He heard her talking under her breath and found her easily. She was sitting on a fallen log trying to take off her boot.

She glanced at him. In the near darkness, he couldn't see her expression. "Can't get these damn things off. My hands are raw from holding so many pairs of reins."

His heart thumped hard at the trust she'd placed in him. Cat Graham didn't let people see her vulnerable or unable to perform a task, much less admit it out loud. James squatted beside her.

"Let me help." He didn't touch her, he simply offered.

"Fine, but don't get 'em wet or I'll never get them back on in the morning." She stuck out her foot.

Her feet were smaller than he expected. With such a big personality, he forgot she was small in stature so naturally she had feet proportionate to her size. He wiggled the boot, which was stuck right good, until it popped off.

"Hell and damnation, that feels good." She yanked off her sock and put her feet in the cool grass.

His body tightened at the moans that popped from her mouth. He pulled the other boot off, then jumped to his feet. She grabbed his hand as he turned to leave.

"You came here for a reason."

It wasn't a question.

"I wanted to check on you. It was a rough day." The words didn't even begin to convey all that had happened since they'd woken that morning.

"It was." She threaded her fingers through his. "Much as I didn't want you here, I'm glad you are."

"Me too."

She gestured to the creek, her arm a blur in the shadows.

"Care to wash up in the water with me?"

He shouldn't. What if Chino decided it was time to pick them off? Danger was around them on all sides. Frolicking with Cat, much as it tempted him, wasn't a wise decision.

"I can't leave you unprotected." He sat down on the log she'd vacated. "I'll watch over you."

"That's no fun."

"It is for me."

She punched his shoulder, hard. "I should tell you to leave."

"You won't."

She paused. "No, I won't."

Cat unbuttoned her shirt, then shed it and dropped it to the ground by her boots. His body reacted to the partial view of her undressing in front of him. Within a minute, she was naked. His dick pressed against the fabric of his trousers.

Cat was sleek, muscled, but curvy as a woman should be. Her breasts could fill his hands. Deep, raw need pulsed through him. He probably shouldn't have offered to watch over her.

What he wanted to do was lay her down in the grass and plunge inside her. Lose himself in the sweet heat of her body.

"Change your mind, cowboy?"

CHAPTER TEN

Cat didn't know how to seduce a man. Even though she'd been intimate with James two days ago, that didn't mean she had intimate knowledge of how to seduce a man, how to be a siren, luring her man into the water with her.

Was James her man?

Or was she letting her heart guide her mind?

Her tumultuous thoughts started her to shaking. She dropped her hands from her hips. If he wasn't interested in her, then she wouldn't make a bigger fool of herself. Cat turned to enter the creek, annoyed and still aroused.

An arm wrapped around her waist and yanked her back against a very hard chest.

"You make it hard to be good." James's husky whisper skated across her ear.

A rush of arousal stole her voice. She tried to wiggle out of his grasp but he held her in place. In the dark, she couldn't anticipate what he would do, and with him behind her, she couldn't see his face.

He cupped her breasts, testing the weight, squeezing with his callused hands. She closed her eyes and leaned against him. His fingers pinched her nipples sending sharp sensations of pleasure through her body.

"That feels good. Do it again."

He chuckled against her ear. "You do have a plain way of talking, Catherine."

"I don't believe in dissembling. If I don't say what I want, I won't get it." She put her hands over his.

The water had cooled her off, but with the first touch of his hands, her temperature had risen. Now she was hot, her body thumping with bubbling passion.

"You're making me all hot and achy." She pushed her ass against his obvious erection behind her. Cat wanted him to put his cock inside her, to show her again what it meant to find the ultimate release.

"You're the one who got naked."

"I needed to wash." She reached behind her to cup him. "Don't you want to get naked too?"

"I can't. Not with Chino and his men twenty feet away." He moved his hand down between her legs. She wasn't embarrassed that he would find her wet. "Jesus, you make it hard to do the right thing."

"That's not the only thing that's hard."

He choked on a laugh. His hand dipped into her pussy and she sucked in a breath. "Let me pleasure you."

"What about you?" Her voice had dropped to a husky whisper.

"Don't worry about me." He circled the bundle of nerves that begged for attention, pinching and rubbing.

She wanted more but she also understood his worry. They were in dangerous company. Cat wasn't a wanton but she sure as hell felt like one at that moment.

He did something with his hand and two fingers slid inside her while he continued to flick her button. He pinched her nipple in time with the movement between her legs.

When she cupped her other breast and repeated his motions, he groaned in her ear.

"Jesus, Cat, you're gonna kill me. That's enough to make me lose control." He kissed her neck, lapping at her skin. When he nibbled her earlobe, her knees grew wobbly.

"It feels too good." The tingles began in her lower belly, spreading downward and out. Small gasps escaped her mouth as she wound tighter and tighter like a coil waiting to spring.

"I can smell you, honey. You're so close, come for me." He pinched her nipple hard and the dam broke within her. She jerked as ripples of ecstasy raced through her. He grabbed her by the waist and held her up. He continued rubbing her pussy, pushing her orgasm further and longer than she thought possible.

Her ears rang and spots danced before her eyes. She sagged against him as the sensations subsided although her heart still pounded. He removed his hand and spun her around. His dark gaze was intense, searching hers.

"You all right?"

She smiled. "I feel good."

He kissed her hard and fast. "Get yourself washed up. I'll stand guard."

"But you—"

"Don't worry about me." He glanced behind him. "I wouldn't wait too long. We've been gone for long enough they're gonna come looking for us."

She wanted to protest, to tell him to strip and continue what he'd started, but she was practical too. Their time alone would come when they were once again free of the mess they'd stepped into.

What happened then was a mystery. Cat hoped both of them would be alive to find out.

It was late morning when they rode up on a rise and James spotted an encampment ahead. His gut tightened although he remained outwardly composed. Time had just run out for James and Cat. They had no option now but to play out the farce they'd been trapped in since they'd run into Chino and his gang.

He wanted to talk to her, to tell her to stay calm and let the sale of the horses happen. They wouldn't find the man behind the theft if they lost control now. Easier said than done, given what he could see of the encampment.

There was a collection of tents scattered in a horseshoe shape and a couple of precarious-looking wooden structures that might pass for shelter if a man was desperate. Several fires burned in and around the camp with curls of smoke rising into the air.

A corral had been constructed to the right and seemed to be the sturdiest thing there. James spotted at least two dozen horses already milling around. This appeared to be a place to buy, sell and trade equines.

He wondered how many of them were stolen. Likely most of them. The camp was something that could be constructed and torn down in less than a day to keep ahead of the law.

"When we get down there, we're done." Chino rode up beside him. "I'm gonna give you what I said I would for you and your crazy woman. She got 'em here alive. They listen to her for some damn reason."

"She has a knack for horses." James looked back at her.

"It's more than that." Chino was far too intelligent to fool completely. "But everybody's got something to hide."

"I suppose that's true." James hid most of who he was from everyone. Cat was the first person who saw the man behind that mask. In truth, she was the first person he allowed to.

He had no idea what was going to happen when they arrived at the camp ahead. They could both be shot, hung or held prisoner. If the lucky stars shone on them, they might even make it out alive.

The last thing he wanted was to meet his end without telling Cat how he felt about her. She had become a part of his life, no matter that he wasn't expecting her or wanted her there. She'd wormed her way into his heart and he thought maybe she was there to stay.

Now he had to figure out what to say to her. What a mess they were in.

"You keep her under control or I'll take care of it myself." Chino left the threat in the air and rode ahead.

James wanted to slow his pace and let the rest of them catch up to him. It might be the only chance he had to talk to Cat. But he wanted to also be on his guard for whatever awaited them in the camp below.

His head versus his heart.

Cat made the decision for him. She came riding up beside him in a flurry of dirt. Her unbound hair fluttered like a golden cloud behind her.

"I left them in charge for a minute. I had to see." She wasn't even breathing hard from the intense ride. She peered down the hill. "You think those horses are stolen too?"

"Maybe." He lowered his voice. "Cat, I need to tell you something—"

"We need to keep to either side of Chino and his men, never together like this. If one of us gets taken, the other can get away." Cat surprised him again. "Keep your hand near your pistol and the other on a knife."

"You sound like we're going to war."

"We are. You're a Texan, aren't you? We're always ready to go to war." She grinned without humor and spun her horse around, galloping out of sight.

He didn't know whether to yell at her or applaud her. He did need to be ready for battle. The truth was, he'd not been in such a dangerous situation with only a woman at his side.

The herd thundered down the hillside, shaking the ground and scattering pebbles. A few folks turned to watch them as they rode closer. Chino was visible by the side of the corral. The big man was talking with a group of others by the corral.

James put his hand on the butt of his pistol while his other hand held tight to the reins. He rode up to Chino and dismounted. James didn't take his eyes off his temporary boss.

The conversation between the other men continued. James backed into the side of the rough-hewn corral fence and watched. Cat dismounted with a leap, her grace astounding. She held tight to the ropes and wrangled the yearlings into the corral with the other horses. She pulled their lead ropes off and let them have a bit of freedom.

Whitey and Al brought the mares in behind Cat. She said something to them James couldn't near and took the mares' ropes from them. The mares and foals followed her like she was the pied piper. Within moments, all the Circle Eight horses were secured in the corral.

James's heart beat a steady tattoo in anticipation. This was it.

Time was up.

Catherine thought she might puke up what little food she'd eaten. Her stomach danced as though the horses were running through her, stomping on her nerves and making her tremble inside. The sad truth was she'd never been in such a situation before.

When she was growing up, she listened to the stories by her sisters and sister-in-law about all the adventures and danger they'd been involved in. Cat resented them for experiencing all of it without her and told herself when she grew up, she would have better adventures.

Now here she was in her own real-life danger and she wanted nothing but to be back home on the Circle Eight. She wouldn't return without her horses and that meant seeing through the situation no matter the consequences.

James seemed as unflappable as always. He stood by his horse, his expression carved from stone. She hoped her own was just as composed. She couldn't swallow and wondered if her lips looked as dry as they felt.

Maybe the puke would moisten her mouth.

A snort tried to escape from her throat. She swallowed it back with effort and ended up belching. Loudly.

Chino turned to look at her. "Damn, woman."

"What? Everyone does it. I can fart too if you want." She decided bravado was the best option considering she wanted to pee herself.

Adventure was not what she thought it would be.

"Jeb, can't you control your woman?" Chino dismissed her as unimportant. That was his mistake.

"I told you she has a mind of her own." James sauntered closer to the big man. "If'n you have a mind to pay us, we can be on our way."

No! I won't leave them. Don't make me leave my babies.

Cat bit her tongue to keep the protests from escaping. She couldn't let them know her desperation. She had to remember she was also angry. Someone took her animals to hurt the Grahams and the Circle Eight.

Her job was not to get herself killed but find out who was behind it and secure the horses. One moment at a time, one breath at a time.

She could do this. She *would* do this.

"Buyer ain't here yet." Chino glanced around. "We gotta wait." He didn't appear too happy about that.

There was a crowd gathered on the far side of the corral, cheering and shouting as two horses flew past side by side. One pulled ahead and half the spectators howled in victory while the others hurled curses at the losing rider.

"Are they racing?" Cat thought the races might help them somehow, although she had no ideas yet. She attempted to sound as though she was curious without being eager.

"They race for the horses. Whoever wins keeps both." This from Whitey. "That's how I won mine."

Cat didn't want to tell him how pitiful his horse was since he seemed so proud of it. Whatever equine he'd raced against must've been a nag. Paladin could destroy any horse in a race.

"You're pretty proud of that gelding of yours." Chino's eyes gleamed with malice. "How about you race and make up for that horse that you put down?"

She bit her tongue to keep the angry words behind her teeth. He'd been the one to kill Starling. She simply put the mare out of her misery.

"She's not racing." James spoke up. "We want to get paid and be on our way."

Too soon. Too soon.

She didn't want to leave her horses yet. She had to find out who was behind the theft and give herself time to grieve for the ones she would have to leave behind.

"You ain't getting a thing until I get paid. He won't be happy we're one horse short." Chino crossed his arms. "You ever race before?"

She nodded. "Yep, but not for money." She wasn't about to tell him that it was usually races against her family. Cat had to maintain the story that she was a drifter without anyone but James.

Whitey snorted. "There ain't no reason to race if'n you're not winning money."

"Or a horse." Chino gestured to Paladin. "Tell you what, if you race and get me another horse, I'll give you an extra two dollars."

Cat wanted to tell him to go to hell, but someone would be an idiot to pass up two dollars. She looked at Whitey. "You heard him. If he reneges, you're my witness."

Whitey grinned a gap-tooth smile. "I heard him. You think you can win?"

"I never lose." She turned to Chino. "Set up the race."

Cat wondered if she'd just set herself to lose her horse. Or possibly her life.

CHAPTER ELEVEN

James wanted to tell her not to race, to keep her at his side where he could keep her safe. Foolish to even want something he knew he could never have. She would do what she wanted to no matter what he thought.

Chino was trying to push her so she'd make a mistake. Offering her money was a ruse. He wanted to see her fail. The big man didn't like her and James wondered if Chino suspected Cat's true identity.

None of it mattered as she led Paladin over to the racecourse. It appeared to be about half a mile long so it was fast and furious. James's gut was stuck somewhere in his throat. Cat walked confidently with her usual swagger, her expression set.

Paladin followed her, his beauty and lines apparent to everyone. The crowd began murmuring the second they spotted him. The hum grew to a roar as they arrived at the starting line.

Chino raised his arms. "Who's up for a race?"

"Is that a woman?"

"She got tits!"

"I'll give her a ride."

James gritted his teeth. He wanted to punch every last one of them. Cat ignored all the comments, her blue eyes like chips of ice.

"Nobody wants to race?" Chino taunted the crowd.

A tall, thin man in stepped forward. He was dressed entirely in black from his hat to his boots. Even his gun belt was black leather. James watched him, noting the way the stranger spoke soft, arranging the race with Chino, much to everyone's delight.

"Anybody want to bet on this match between Katie and

Duffy, come see me. Race starts in ten minutes." Chino grinned as he was surrounded by people who wanted to make some money on the race.

James stepped up beside Cat. "Are you sure about this?"

"There isn't another choice." She glanced at her opponent. "Besides, that man isn't any competition. A stiff breeze could knock him over."

James glanced at the man called Duffy. He hid his face in the shadows beneath the black hat. He wasn't a big man and he rode a paint. The smaller horse was little competition against Paladin, who was bred for speed and endurance.

"Don't hurt him."

She managed a small smile. "I'll behave."

"No you won't." He squeezed her hand. "I didn't think I'd ever say this, but be careful."

She blinked. "Are you concerned about me?"

"I, uh, yeah." His cheeks burned and he hoped like hell he wasn't blushing. It wasn't the time to tell Cat he cared about her. He hadn't figured it all out yet.

"Oh." She turned to look at her opponent. "I'll try not to win by too much. Don't want to embarrass him."

He kissed her quick. "Good luck."

She nodded, then went to work checking Paladin's saddle. As she led him to the starting line, her opponent did the same. The crowd grew louder with each passing second. The frenzy built as she mounted her horse.

"Show her how a man races, Duffy!"

"She'll get a ride on her twat!"

"Hey, will she ride Duffy after the race?"

Guffaws, snorts and more cursing than James had ever heard in his life followed. It felt as if a thousand ants were marching up and down his skin. He hadn't known what the urge to protect what was his or deep-wrenching jealousy were until this moment.

He wanted to snatch her off that horse and ride off, forget the horses and the need to find out who wanted to hurt the Grahams. None of it was more important than her life.

Or the fact that he loved her.

James could only stand there amongst the crowd and watch as

the riders exchanged a few words. They shook hands, then Cat spoke again. After Duffy responded they nodded and faced forward, their hands gripping the reins.

When the shot rang out Paladin surged forward with the other rider's horse hot on his heels. They were almost neck and neck the entire race. James chanted under his breath.

"C'mon, Cat, faster, faster, faster. I know that horse has wings."

Cat was leaned over Paladin's neck, likely whispering in his ear, as they moved as one being. Her opponent was doing the same, the man almost as graceful as Cat. It was half-mile course and James couldn't see the actual finish line.

The horses were side by side from what he could see. The urge to know overtook him and he ran along the side of the course. The crowd erupted as the horses crossed the finish line.

He cursed as he got caught up in the surge of onlookers and had to elbow, punch, kick and curse his way through the mass of bodies. Many of which hadn't been acquainted with a bar of soap in quite some time.

James finally reached the end to find Cat and her opponent shaking hands. Relief coursed through James when she saw him and gave him a small smile. The man called Duffy handed her the reins to the paint and took the saddle and blanket. He walked through the crowd with his head held high. That man could ride like the wind.

"And the winner, Katie!" Chino pointed to Whitey. "All bets settled here." He took the reins of the paint from Cat and walked away with it.

Cat shook her head and threw herself back up on Paladin. The catcalls and whistles followed as she made her way to James. When she reached him, he swung up behind her and they rode back toward the corral.

"Did you give them a show? Or was that man as good as he looked?"

She shrugged. "People are never what they seem. Duffy was good. Real good. I had to fight to win that race." She patted Paladin's neck. "I almost lost but this boy saved me."

James wasn't sure if they should celebrate a victory or not. Chino no doubt had an ulterior motive for encouraging Cat to race. They had to protect themselves until they figured out what.

The afternoon passed slowly. Cat swore the air shimmered with tension as they all found ways not to look at each other. Men walked past her every so often. Some tipped their hats. Most of them sneered or murmured something that made James growl.

It was one of the most uncomfortable and excruciatingly long days she could remember. That included the times they had to dig a new outhouse hole at the Circle Eight. It smelled almost as bad though. The stench surrounding the camp was rather fierce.

Just when she thought she would lose what was left of her sanity, two men rode up to where Chino leaned against the corral fence. He greeted the man in a low voice. Cat sauntered closer to overhead their conversation. James hissed at her but she ignored him. He followed her, standing close enough she could feel him nearby.

The stranger had light brown hair and blue eyes. He was shorter than Chino, with a slender build and delicate features. She would call him pretty if she didn't think he might pull that shiny pistol out and shoot her. Or the giant behind him might.

The man traveled with a bodyguard, one that looked as fierce and cold as any gunslinger. Not that she'd ever seen one, but again the stories she'd grown up hearing echoed through her head. The man was dangerous, as was his employer.

The danger around them increased tenfold. If this man was the buyer, he definitely had money. Lots of it.

His clothes were impeccable, with tight stitches and hidden seams. Made by someone who was an expert seamstress, perhaps even brought in from a far off place like New York. Or Paris.

The bodyguard held the reins of the horses behind the fancy man. One of them had the fanciest saddle she'd ever seen in her life. The tooling must've taken a week and the conchos shone in the sun with turquoise insets. The man's boots were just as intricate as the leather on the saddle. He pulled a cigar from his shirt pocket, an embroidered shirt pocket, and lit a match on the corral fence post.

As he puffed on the cigar, the stranger glanced at Cat. His gaze was colder than the ice in January and she pinched her arm to stop the shiver from escaping. Something about him struck a chord within her but she couldn't say what or why. Perhaps it was the darkness that glimmered from behind his eyes.

"Who is this?" His voice was deeper than she expected.

"Hired hand."

"Not many women work as hired hands."

"I'm not many women." She leaned against Paladin, hiding the brand. Her instincts told her to disguise anything that tied her to the Circle Eight from this man. The small hairs on her arms stood at attention and what she thought was fear before now turned into icy terror dancing up her spine.

This was the man responsible for the thefts. She was certain of it.

"I can see that." He smiled and she bumped into the horse, trying to move farther away. Paladin tossed his head and smacked her in the face with his tail.

"Beautiful horse for a hired hand."

She bared her teeth. "Amazing what you can find when you look for it."

He raised his brows. "I couldn't agree more."

"Are we doing business or are you going to fuck her?" Chino interrupted with an impatient huff of breath. "If you don't want 'em I'm sure I can find someone who does."

"Annoying me does not do you any good." The man flicked his gaze to Chino. "If you push me, I push back." He caressed the butt of his pistol.

Chino scoffed. "I did the job. Your man counted the horses so you got what you need."

"Nino counted one less than what I ordered."

There was a pause. "One of the mares didn't make it. I got a paint to replace her."

"Is that so?" The man toed the dirt with his fancy boot. Cat couldn't take her eyes from him. "I didn't pay you to kill a horse. I paid you to bring them to me. If I wanted a paint, a *male* one, I would've told you that."

"I did what you asked. It ain't my fault that damn horse got sick." Chino apparently didn't want any blame for his stupidity because he pointed at her. "She put the mare down."

The stranger turned his attention back to Cat. "And how did

you do this deed, *chica?*"

She pulled the knife from its scabbard on her back. The metal glinted in the sun. "Quietly."

He stepped closer, puffing on his cigar. The sickly sweet smell made her stomach roll. Puking might occur whether she wanted it or not.

"*¿Como se llama, chica?*"

"Katie."

His eyes were empty. She'd never seen walking evil, perhaps didn't believe in it. Until now.

"Katie, my name is Manfred Cunningham."

He spoke as though the name would trigger a response from her. She stood stock still, not even blinking. The name was unfamiliar regardless.

"And I'm Jeb. Her husband." James stepped up beside her, his jaw tight and his hand on the pistol with whitened knuckles.

"Husband?" Mr. Cunningham stepped back. "I didn't know a, ah, delicate flower such as yourself would snare a man. I thought perhaps you could be trained and groomed."

Her pride smarted. "I'm not a horse, mister."

"All women are like horses. It's all in how they're trained." He turned back to Chino.

She wanted to shoot the fancy man. More than once.

"Easy," James spoke between his teeth. "It's almost over."

She held tight to her emotions as they ran riot through her. Whoever Manfred Cunningham was, she held him responsible for the theft and the deaths of Starling and her baby. She would do whatever was necessary to make sure he paid.

A man walked to the right of the corral but she didn't pay attention to him. She kept her gaze locked on Cunningham as he spoke to Chino, low enough for no one to hear the conversation.

She memorized all the details she could see. If nothing else, she could give the information to the Rangers and they could go after the man. It wasn't what she *wanted* to do, but it was what she *could* do.

When the unholy howl split the air, she jumped a foot in the air. A body flew toward Mr. Cunningham and slammed into him.

It was her brother Ben.

CHAPTER TWELVE

There were times in her life that Cat remembered with vivid clarity. The smells, the sights, the tastes and even more so, how she felt. It could be joy or annoyance, excitement or curiosity.

The moment she saw her brother streak through the air toward Manfred Cunningham and the blood began to fly, she was painfully aware of every second.

The sound of Ben's inhuman howls, the scent of blood, the sound of the men murmuring as they watched, the feel of the sun's warmth on her shoulders, and the taste of the fear on her tongue.

Sweet Lord have mercy.

Mere seconds passed before she gained control of her reaction. Ben's fist flew again and again, smashing into the other man's face with the sickening crunch of bones.

"Ben, stop it!" She threw herself on his back, but she might as well have been a fly the way he flicked her off. Her teeth slammed together when she landed on the ground, skidding a few feet.

She looked at James, who watched open mouthed. "Stop him!"

"How? Do you want me to shoot him?" He moved in close to Ben's arm as it pistoned up and down. It clipped his shoulder and James stumbled backward.

Cat jumped to her feet and landed on Ben's back again. "Stop, stop, stop!" She didn't realize she was crying until a salty tear crept into the corner of her mouth. He paused and she put all her weight into pulling him.

They tumbled sideways and Cat landed hard on her shoulder,

but she still had hold of his arm.

"Let me go!" He rolled to his knees and yanked, but she held fast. He shook her hard enough to make her bones rattle.

Cat hung on. Something told her if she let go, she was allowing him to lose whatever shred of Ben was left. Tears continued to roll down her face into the dirt breath her.

"Benjy."

He sucked in a breath that sounded more like a sob. "Let me go, Kitty."

His voice caught on the childhood nickname he'd used, the secret name only the two of them knew. She knew he could use brute force to free his arm, but he didn't.

"Never." She wrapped her arms around him and his head dropped to her shoulder. He shook with silent sobs as she held him. Her throat was so tight, she couldn't swallow.

Jesus, what had just happened?

She ignored the men who spoke above them and rocked her brother. Something horrible had just occurred. She would let them see to Mr. Cunningham. He'd no doubt need a doctor after the vicious beating Ben had given him.

James squatted down beside her. A smear of dirt decorated on his cheek and the brim of his hat was crooked. Ben must've hit him harder than she thought.

"He's dead." James's words hit her like a punch.

"What?" Her voice had dropped to a whisper.

"Cunningham is dead. His bodyguard doesn't seem too put out, but he was grumbling about being paid. Same as Chino." James looked behind him. "One of them is going to be over here wanting to know who this is and why he just beat another man to death."

The stark truth that her brother had killed someone in front of her, and numerous other witnesses, sent a frisson of dread down her spine. This wasn't like him. He wasn't a murderer. Yet he'd just killed a man.

"Fucking hell." She closed her eyes. "They're going to try to hang him."

"That would be my guess." James gestured to Ben. "Is he making any sense?"

She shook her head. "We need to get him out of here."

"What about the horses?"

"Forget the horses." She didn't even hesitate. Nothing, *nothing*, was more important than her family. Than Benjamin.

"Let's get him up and start moving before someone realizes what we're doing." James blocked the others' view as they got Ben to his feet and walked toward Paladin. The horse could carry both of them if she asked him to. She had no idea where Ben's horse was, but it didn't matter. They needed to move. To escape.

Cat thought she'd left the ranch to rescue the horses that were stolen from her. While she'd left the Circle Eight to rescue the horses stolen from her, it was now clear she needed to rescue her brother more. She was the youngest girl, but Ben was her little brother. It was her duty to save him, no matter what.

She rushed toward Paladin and whistled under her breath. The horse's ears perked up and he stomped a front hoof. He loved to race and her signal to be ready was a godsend today. She trained her horses but she was never so grateful to have done so than at this moment.

"Get up on the saddle, Ben." She pushed at him as he climbed. Cat threw herself in front of him and pulled the reins hard to the left. Paladin flew into motion.

She could only hope that James was right behind her. His gelding, Bernie, was as fast as hers. She had to think about Ben first. No matter how much she had fallen in love with James Gibson.

Her heart stuttered.

Was she in love with James? Cat knew what love was, but she didn't know what being in love was. Until now apparently. With more strength than she knew she possessed, Cat pushed aside thoughts of loving James.

Surviving the next five minutes had to be her focus. She expected a bullet in the back or the sound of horses chasing them. All she heard was the wind in her ears, the sound of Paladin's hooves hitting the ground and the strange noises from Ben. More like whispers she couldn't understand than whimpers or crying. He'd wrapped his arms around her waist, but he wasn't quite holding on.

She was scared for him. Not just for the potential posse that might hunt them down, but because he had just killed a man.

And she thought, perhaps, also killed a piece of himself.

One thing was for certain. If she hadn't chased after the horses alone, Ben would have never followed her or murdered a man.

Cat's life would never be the same.

James kept glancing over his shoulder but, to his surprise, no one followed them. The last thing he'd seen was Chino going through the dead man's pockets on one side and the bodyguard doing the same on the other.

It made James sick to his stomach. Cat would never know why Cunningham had hired Chino to steal the horses. Nor would they get them back. The Grahams' blood stock would be decimated for future generations. It was the worst possible outcome outside of their own deaths.

James had to agree that Cat had made the right choice to pull Ben out of there. Those men would have hung him for his crime. That encampment was teeming with the type of people who would go through a dead man's pockets, steal his boots and throw his corpse in a ditch for the carrion eaters.

They were also the type of people to hang someone without a lawman to stop them if they thought he'd committed a crime. Especially a crime like murder or horse thievery.

The truth was, Ben had committed a crime. He'd beaten a man to death. James had never seen such a thing before. Using a fist was much different than shooting someone. By that measure, a bullet was impersonal.

This death was very personal. If James had to hazard a guess, Ben knew Cunningham and the beating had nothing to do with the horse theft. James had met the youngest Graham when they were both half-grown and had always liked him. He had a darkness in his soul, that was certain, but he wasn't violent by nature.

Something had pushed him to it today.

Or some*one*.

They raced south for at least half an hour. Cat led them into a wooded area to lose any pursuers.

"Are they following?" Cat shouted into the wind.

"No. Nothing back there." James eased up on the reins. "We

should rest the horses."

She kept darting around the trees, ignoring him. He shouldn't be surprised. Cat had her own way of doing things. An understatement of course.

"Cat! Paladin needs water." He had to shout to be heard.

She glanced around and must've realized he wasn't behind her any longer. She patted Ben's leg and then turned Paladin around. As she rode toward him, she kept her gaze on the open ground behind them.

Her face was flushed and her eyes hard. Ben was slumped behind her. Although his arms circled her waist, he hid his face in her shoulder. His knuckles were bloodied and raw, slowly dripping onto Cat's trousers.

James would never forget the sight of one man killing another with his fists. Every time he looked at Ben, he would remember it. That's not how he wanted to think of his friend, but James knew his memory couldn't be erased.

Nothing would be the same for the three of them again.

"Why didn't they follow?" Her breath was choppy while her hair was a frizzy, knotted braid on her shoulder.

"They were too busy stripping the body of his worldly goods." James scowled. "Including his own bodyguard. Since Cunningham was about to pay Chino for the horses, I expect he had the money somewhere on his person."

"Chino is a pig."

"I'm not going to argue with you."

Cat wasn't scared or upset. She was furious. "Not only did they steal our fucking horses, but now we'll never get them back and we'll never know what happened to them."

"I'm sorry," Ben's muffled reply made her twitch.

"You didn't make them steal our herd, Benjy." She blew out a breath. "Let's give the horses some water and then get moving. We'll keep it to a walk for a bit."

James dismounted, as did Cat, but Ben stayed as he was. They used the water from their canteens to see to the horses. Things were quiet in the shade of the trees. He wanted to comfort Cat but didn't know how.

"Benjy, you're going to have to come back to us." She held up the canteen for her brother.

"Not thirsty."

She snorted. "That's a load of horse shit. Now drink."

James almost forgot that the big man on the horse was Cat's little brother. She knew how to order him around and it worked. Ben took the canteen and poured some water into his mouth. Half of it slid down his chin, but he didn't wipe it.

Cat took the canteen back and quenched her own thirst. James hadn't recognized just how much she took care of everyone, and everything, around her. She wasn't the selfish brat he first thought she was.

No, Cat was a woman who showed the world how to care for others. James had never taken care of anyone but himself. Occasionally he watched his brother Will but that was for a few hours at a time and they usually did something fun, like skip rocks or play checkers.

He'd never had to be responsible. Or perhaps he had never been adult enough to step forward and take the reins. It was humbling and almost painful. He wanted to be more like Cat. She was the adult he should strive to be.

She hung the canteen back on the saddle and met his gaze. He saw a myriad of emotions in her beautiful blue eyes. James opened his arms and she flew into them.

Her body was hot and sticky but he didn't care. They could stink together. He rubbed her back while she trembled. He didn't know if she was crying or if the last hour had stripped away the crusty shell she carried like a shield against the world.

"I'm sorry, honey." He kissed the top of her head.

"I wish things were different."

"I don't."

She leaned back to scowl at him.

"If things were different you might not be in my arms. We might never have gone past that first kiss." His heart slammed against his ribs and the rest of the words danced on the end of his tongue.

Tell her.

"I reckon that's true." She snuggled beneath his chin.

He was able to pull in a breath.

Tell her.

"Mistakes are things that move us in one direction or another.

Choices do the same thing." Words tumbled from his mouth.

Tell her.

"You sound like a book." She was right, of course.

Tell her.

"I wanted to tell you what I was thinking. And…" His mouth stopped working again.

"And?"

"I love you, Catherine."

She started and grew very still. "What?"

"I don't know how or why it happened, but there it is. I love you." Now the words flowed. He'd yanked the cork of fear that had been clogging his life for years.

"I… That is… You do?" She finally leaned back and he saw wonder in her eyes this time.

He smiled. "I do."

She tightened her arms around him and nearly climbed him like a tree, pressing her cheek against his. "Holy shit."

His heart opened and what he experienced was no longer pain. It was joy, love and the sweetness of having found the one person who was meant to be his.

Cat had never felt so out of control. Frightened, angry and confused had just turned into happy and joyful. Or possibly a mixture of all of them. James had told her that he loved her.

Now she had to find the courage to tell him the same. She clung to him, the anchor in the sea of craziness in which she swam.

Her brother sat unmoving on Paladin's saddle. Her happiness was tempered by the seriousness of the situation and her worry for Ben.

James kissed her forehead and released her from the circle of his arms. "Talk to him."

She nodded and summoned up the strength of a Graham and returned to Ben's side. She patted his knee, hiding her distress over the steady drip of blood from his ravaged hands.

"Ben, you need to let me clean and wrap your hands. You know Rebecca would be screeching at us if we didn't take care of wounds."

He shook his head.

"There's no call to punish yourself. Done is done. Now please let me be your sister and take care of you." She held her breath and, to her relief, he swung down from the saddle.

Cat was by no means petite, but standing between her brother and James made her feel small in stature. She retrieved the canteen again and poured some water over Ben's wounds, willing him to talk.

"I remember Mama doing this very thing to my knee when I was little. I don't have many recollections of her, but this was one of them. She wiped my eyes with her handkerchief and snuck me a peppermint." Ben's voice was barely above a whisper.

Cat smiled. "She did the same when I scraped myself up. I think she had a stash of them for that purpose."

"I did a bad thing, Kitty."

She blinked away the stinging in her eyes and looked at him steadily. "Yes, you did."

"He was a bad person. Really bad."

She retrieved a spare neckerchief from her saddlebags to tear into strips before she spoke. The last thing she wanted to do was spook him. "You knew him."

Ben nodded. "Manfred."

Cat's heart picked up speed. She saw a blackness in Ben's expression she'd never seen before. Since he'd returned to the family at age ten, having been kidnapped at five, he had always kept himself hidden away. Never letting anyone see beneath, never telling anyone of his five years captivity by Pablo Garza. Caleb had killed the man after rescuing Ben.

There was so much more to the story though. And it must involve Mr. Cunningham. She wrapped Ben's knuckles, wincing for him as she did. He needed stitches, but they had no time and no supplies to do it.

"He was the trainer."

Cat stopped and glanced up at her brother. "Pardon?"

"Manfred was the trainer for the new boys Pablo brought into the house. He taught them how to please Pablo." Ben's tone was so light he could have been talking about shoeing his horse.

She swallowed the lump in her throat. "He trained you."

"He did. I was an apt pupil but he liked me so much he kept

me for longer. He told Pablo I needed extra help." Ben's eyes had become stones, hard and emotionless.

"How long?" She could hardly force the words out.

"Manfred kept me for a year. He trained me to be and do whatever he wanted." Ben stepped away from her, the end of the makeshift bandage on his left hand trailing. "Even after I became Pablo's, Manfred would come by to see me. He told me he missed me."

Cat didn't know what to do or say. Beating that man to death was too good for him. She wanted to shoot him and hang him too. Possibly even set the fucker on fire.

"Do you think he was angry at us for taking you back? It's been over ten years." She didn't understand the twisted workings of a mind like Cunningham's.

"He wasn't there when Caleb and Rory found me. Who knows what he heard or knew about Pablo's death. He might have been searching for me and finally found a way to cause pain."

"Because he was in pain? That's ridiculous." Cat frowned. "What pain did we cause him?"

"You took his favorite toy."

Bile coated the back of Cat's throat. She swallowed it back, unwilling to let Ben see how much his words had affected her.

Ben turned back to Cat. This time his eyes brimmed with unshed tears, the naked agony shone brightly. "I killed him."

She pulled him into a hug and held him tight while his body shook with silent sobs. This was her little brother. The scamp she spent all her time with as a little girl. They had been closer than any of their other siblings as small children. Rebecca became her best friend, but there was always a hole in her life from the loss of Ben, no matter that he eventually came back. Benjy was gone. When he'd been taken, she'd felt like half of her was missing.

Now she knew she'd never get that half back.

"We need to go to Brody and Caleb, talk to the Rangers." Their brother-in-law and their brother were both ex-Texas Rangers.

"No." Ben straightened up and rid himself of any residual tears from his cheeks with angry swipes. "I can't go back to the Circle Eight and I can't go to prison. I've got to disappear."

"No." She grabbed his arm. "I won't let you."

"It's not your choice. I've got to go." He looked at her horse. "I need Paladin."

Her heart was surely breaking into a thousand pieces. She shook her head. "No, Ben. I can't." She couldn't lose Benjy again.

"You have to." He took her saddlebags and set them on the ground. Then he spoke to James. "You get her back safely."

"There's no other option." James, the traitor, held out his hand and Ben shook it. "Godspeed."

"If there is a God, he doesn't care a damn thing about me." Ben hugged Cat hard and fast. He threw himself into the saddle. "My horse is staked in the woods west of that camp. He's tied to a tree so he'll need someone to take care of him."

Cat cried openly now, her heart lying on the ground at her feet. "Benjy."

"Love you, Kitty." With that he was gone, Paladin's powerful muscles carrying him farther and farther away.

James once again wrapped his arms around her and safe within his warmth, she let herself weep.

CHAPTER THIRTEEN

After Ben left, James and Cat stayed in the small wooded area for another fifteen minutes, until her tears subsided and her shaking became an occasional tremble. Ben had done the right thing by leaving his sister. He was guilty, not her, and she needed to return home to her family, horses or not.

James wasn't about to tell Cat his opinion, but he silently thanked Ben for making it. The man had great courage inside and out. James didn't know about Ben's childhood or that he'd been kept prisoner by a sick bastard like Cunningham and whoever Pablo Garza was. James was surprised Ben hadn't lost what was left of his mind already. Damn sure wouldn't blame him.

"I let him go. Alone. When he was bleeding and lost inside." Cat pressed her hands to her face. "How can I face my family?"

He pulled her hands away. "By telling them the truth. Ben is an adult who made his choice. Your family will understand."

"How can they when I don't?" She had never looked so vulnerable.

He took her hands in his. "You don't have to understand or explain why Ben did what he did. It was his choice. He's a grown man."

"He's my little brother."

James squeezed her fingers. "You think I had any control over Will before the accident?" He snorted. "Hell no. He made decisions and what happened after that was all on him, good or bad."

She frowned. "Why do you sound so smart all of a sudden?"

He raised a brow. "You don't think I'm smart?"

"You know what I mean. Your family isn't exactly ideal

either." She shrugged. "I guess we were meant to bump into each other."

"What makes you so romantic all of a sudden?" He was rewarded by one of her laughs, that tinkling melody.

"Since I met you."

She pressed her lips together and pressed her forehead to his shoulder. She didn't speak, but he could feel the ripples between them. It was all so new, he didn't even know how to act around her.

Their love was too new, too fragile. He didn't want to talk about it too long or leave it where it could break.

"Do you want to go back for Ben's horse?" James sure as hell didn't want to return to that camp but he would do it. For her.

"He'll get himself loose eventually." Her tone was faraway.

James held her away from him and scowled. "This from the master of horses? You would let that animal suffer?"

A bit of spark glimmered in her blue eyes. "That's not what I said."

"No, you said he would get himself loose. When that happened, if it did, it would have been long after he needed water. And he'd be wandering around with all that tack on and no one to take care of him." James was being dramatic but he wanted to snap her out of the grief that had enfolded her in its dark wings.

"Fine. We can ride up through the other side and into the wooded area. Maybe wait until the sun starts to set and it'll be behind us. Then they might not recognize us." She pressed her hand to her cheeks. "I don't know my ass from a hole in the ground right now."

"Then it's lucky I'm here to take care of you and your ass." He kissed her, the very taste of her bringing him back into the here and now. "The important thing now is to get home safe. Bernie is strong but he's not going to be able to carry both us at any speed but walking all the way back to the Circle Eight."

"You're right. Damn it." She cupped his cheek. "I never thought I'd say this, but I want to go home."

He wanted to ask her about the stolen horses, but didn't. Her emotions were raw and he didn't know how to help her except to keep her focused on one thing at a time. First, getting Ben's horse back.

They mounted his gelding and went in a roundabout path back toward the encampment. The hills provided landmarks to get them where they needed to be. His nerves were stretched tight as a bowstring waiting for someone to find them, see them, shoot at them.

Cat rode behind him, her arms firmly around his waist, the only bright spot in the last hour. They had an hour until the sun began to set. He wanted to find a vantage point to watch the encampment and find out what had happened after they'd galloped away.

If he was right, they'd thrown Cunningham's body into a hole after divvying up his belongings. Including the stolen horses from the Circle Eight.

"You see anything?" She peered around his shoulder toward the camp.

"Nothing unusual. Nobody's got pitchforks or torches." He patted her leg. "Why don't you get down and we can give the horse a rest."

She dismounted and waited while he joined her. The camp was far enough away all they could see was figures moving around and horses milling in the corral. A few gray columns of smoke rose lazily into the late-day sky from cooking fires. It looked almost normal.

James knew different. The men that were there were more like a pack of wolves, waiting for the weakest one to falter so they could pick its bones. No matter what Ben had done, he wasn't like them. The man James knew had endured horrors, that was obvious, but in his heart he was a good person who'd done something terrible.

He knew Cat was worried about Ben, but he'd meant what he told her. It had been Ben's choice to leave. When he needed his family, they would be there for him. James hoped like hell that would happen sooner than later.

The sun crept down the horizon, bathing the ground in splashes of radiant colors. James untied the horse's reins from the branch.

"Let's go." They walked the horse through the woods until the open field between the treed areas. James told himself they were dots on the horizon and no one could see them. His stomach was tight and he wondered how long it would be before he could eat again.

The sounds from the camp echoed across the tall grass and he used every ounce of self-control not to look. He couldn't turn to Cat either. He had no doubt she was staring straight ahead, unwilling to risk being caught.

When they were ten feet from the trees, he spotted Ben's horse. They were close enough to hear it nicker in response to Bernie's greeting. A shadow darted behind the tree near the gelding.

"Shit."

"What's wrong?" Cat's voice was barely above a whisper.

"There's someone there and I don't think it's Ben."

Cat crouched down when they reached the edge of the trees. She crept forward into the forest, gun in hand, while she tried to locate the figure James had seen. Whoever it was must not want to make their presence known to the camp either, or they wouldn't be creeping around in the woods.

James had gone around to the right and Cat to the left. As she moved deeper into the trees, she noted there were plenty of dead leaves left from the previous fall, but they'd been soaked by rains the last few weeks. Soundless and soft.

She stayed upwind of the horse, but he stomped his hoof, aware another animal was close. Ben had named him Kick to pay homage to his pony from long ago, Kickers. Kick had a white blaze on the left side of his nose, a cousin to Paladin. Ben always said the horse was slightly off center, just like his owner.

She pushed aside memories and the rush of emotion at the thought of her brother. She needed to act like a Graham, not a female.

The snick of the gun beside her ear sent a lightning bolt of fear through her before she grabbed it by the tail. She didn't turn her head or even blink.

"You better plan on using that or I'll use mine."

A chuckle. "Balls of steel. I knew I liked you." The voice was unfamiliar.

"I like her too. Matter of fact, I love her. That means I blow a

hole in your head if you so much as fart in her direction."
James's pronouncement made Cat bare her teeth. Damn, he was
good. "Now get up, stranger."

Cat jumped to her feet, gun in hand. James stood there
looking like an avenging angel with dark brown hair and several
days' growth of whiskers. She stared at the person who'd snuck
up on her.

"Duffy?"

She'd spoken to the man before and after the race, but she
hadn't thought of him since. He wore the same black clothes.
She couldn't see the color of his hair beneath the hat but she did
see what she thought were dark green eyes. Now that she was
within two feet of him without her nerves dancing up and down
her spine, she was able to see what she'd missed before.

Delicate features, *feminine* ones. "Holy shit. You're a
woman."

The corner of Duffy's mouth quirked up. "Most of 'em don't
even notice. You're the first."

"Duffy? A woman?" James peered at the stranger. "You're
the one who lost the race."

"I did." Duffy rocked back on her heels. "It seemed to me
your wife needed to win that race. Believe me, Chino can't be
trusted. He's a thief, a liar and a murderer. He shows up every
month with a passel of horses and sells 'em to Cunningham.
Both of them aren't worth a spit."

Cat wasn't surprised to hear about the leader of the thieves.
The man had malice embedded in his bones. "Cunningham's
dead. I guess that means Chino lost his regular buyer."

"That he did. It took him about ten minutes before he realized
it. Then after he cussed up a storm, he went looking for the
stranger who killed Cunningham." Duffy paused, her eyes
guarded. "Then he was looking for you two."

Cat met James's gaze. He was frowning hard enough to make
his brows almost touch.

"You here to bring us back?" James didn't let loose of his
pistol. If anything, his hand tightened until his knuckles turned
white.

"No. I'm here to warn you."

Cat stepped back a few more feet from Duffy. "You pulled a

gun on me. Why would you do that and then warn me?"

"You were fixing to kick my ass. I had to do something to stop you before one of us got hurt. Besides, not too many women wear trousers like me. You also ride better than any man I've ever seen and your horse loves you." Duffy folded her arms. "Someone who takes care of their animal to that point is a friend of mine."

Cat didn't expect to find a friend in the midst of the chaos she was swimming in. She didn't have many friends outside her family. Most women shied away from Cat because of her ways, her dress and her obsession with horses.

"I don't know if I want a friend." No one could say she didn't speak her mind. Cat had a tendency to blurt words before her brain caught up with her.

"Fair enough. But know that I can help you get your horses back." Duffy let that hang in the air. "I recognized you the moment I saw your face. You're a Graham. Those horses Chino delivered belong to your family's ranch."

"Fucking hell." Cat couldn't protect herself. Chino would hunt Cat if he found out who she was. "We could kill you now and be done with it."

Duffy shook her head. "You won't do that."

"She might not, but I would." James wore an icy mask of ferocity. It sent a shiver up Cat's spine.

Duffy held up her hands. "I'm not here to sell you to Chino. I want to hurt him until he squeals like a little girl. I want him to piss himself in fear before he gets sent to hell."

"What did he do to you?" Cat peered at the other woman but her expression was guarded beneath the brim of her hat.

After a brief hesitation, Duffy appeared to let her true motion show. "He stole horses from my husband and then shot him dead when he tried to stop Chino's band of dogs." Her voice now shook with rage. It echoed through Cat. This she understood. This she respected.

"How long ago?"

"A year. I hunted Chino until I found him. I've been waiting for my chance to make him pay. Taking his life is too easy. I want him to suffer." Duffy's smile was frightening. "You two helped me and so did the man who killed Cunningham."

Cat knew what it meant to seek revenge against those who hurt her family. The man she traveled with, the man she had fallen in love with, had hurt her family years earlier. Yet she'd forgiven him. He was a good person in his heart and he'd been a boy when he'd burned the Circle Eight.

Chino was not a boy. He was an evil man who had been stealing horses, killing and wreaking havoc for at least a year. And apparently he'd murdered Duffy's husband.

"Are you wearing your husband's clothes?" Cat asked.

"It's all I have left of him. It keeps me close to him even though he's gone. After he died, I lost everything but what I could carry. Thanks to you, I lost the horse I won in a race last month." Duffy glanced toward the camp. "The paint was good but not like your magnificent creature."

Cat had a choice to make. She could trust this strange woman and take a chance. Or they could tie her up and run like hell. Duffy was right about one thing. Cat wouldn't kill her.

"Who was the man?" Duffy interrupted her thoughts.

Cat frowned. "What man?"

"The one who killed Cunningham. I didn't get a good look at him because I was on the other side of the corral." Duffy narrowed her gaze. "He left with you. Now he's gone and so is your other horse. This one belonged to Cunningham's killer."

Cat winced at the description of Ben as a killer. Regardless of what he'd done, he wasn't a cold-blooded murderer.

"Who the hell *are* you?" James growled. "Is there anything you don't notice?"

Duffy shrugged. "I've spent the last year watching people. Observing how they act, how they talk, how they make choices. You two are good people in a bad situation."

"How are you going to help us get away?" James sounded frustrated. "And get the Circle Eight horses back?"

"I ride past the camp in Katie's clothes, shooting in the air, and then ride north. I've got a ride nearby that can pass for your horse at a distance. You come in after, get your horses and head south." Duffy was suggesting she sacrifice herself for two strangers.

It didn't add up.

Duffy took off her hat and the black cloth covering her hair.

Long blonde hair tumbled down. Cat stared at the other woman, surprised to find Duffy could pass for Cat from a distance in the right clothes.

"Damn." Cat shook her head. "What do you want in return?" Cat waited while Duffy stared off in the distance.

"I want my revenge. The man who helped you. He can help me." Duffy's cold rage was back, her eyes chips of green stone. "If you tell me who he is and something only you would know, I'll convince him to pay me back for helping you two escape."

Cat couldn't find any logic in the plan. They had little choice but to trust her. If she was right, Cat and James could escape with their lives and the horses.

"We'll do it."

James knew it was a bad idea. They should have just ridden away as quietly as they could. Then Duffy had to show up. The woman who'd disguised herself as a man for a year. Her ability to blend in and sit on her revenge like she was cooking an egg of hellfire was impressive. And frightening.

He wanted to hightail it out of there. He also wanted to protect Cat, but the truth was that Duffy's plan was solid. Getting Chino to chase her was madness, but the woman was cold as ice. She was an odd one. Now that she had removed the hat, he was surprised to discover she was attractive. The woman was a chameleon.

James pulled Cat aside. "Are you sure about this?"

Cat made a face. "No, but if she can help us get the horses back, it's worth it."

"We'll have to ride like hell to outrun them. What about the foals?" James knew she wouldn't risk the babies. They damn sure couldn't run like a full-grown horse, nor could the pregnant mares.

She frowned. "We'll have to leave the mares and the foals and just take the yearlings. I hate to do it but if we try to run with all of them, they'll die or we'll all die." Agony contorted her features. "I don't want to abandon them."

He pulled her into his arms. "You tell me what you want to do and I'll do it. This is your decision."

No matter what he would make sure Cat made it home safe

and alive. His promise to Eva and Hannah aside, James would die protecting her. She'd become the other half of himself. He couldn't imagine going back to his room at the livery and not sleeping beside her every night.

"We could split up."

"No." His answer was fast and hard. "There is no goddamn way we are splitting up."

"If we don't take the foals, they'll be sold. If we just take the mares, the foals won't be able to nurse. The others might lose their foals before they're born safely." Cat pressed her forehead against his shoulder. "This is breaking my heart."

A week ago, she wouldn't have told him what time it was if he'd asked. Now she was showing her vulnerability, her love of the horses, and the real Cat beneath the rough clothes. His throat tightened with softer emotions he'd not allowed himself to have before. She was beautiful inside and out.

"The yearlings, then?"

"Fuck. Fuck. Fuck." She pushed away from him. "I suppose bringing the yearlings back is better than returning without any of them."

"They can also run a lot faster than the foals and the pregnant mares." He was always thinking of the worst in a situation.

Cat's expression fell. "I won't get to see their babies born." Her hand crept to her gun. "I hope Duffy finds a way to get her revenge on Chino. If she doesn't, I will."

"Let's get home safe and then worry about that." James hadn't been a believer in the Texas Rangers, but meeting Caleb, Cat's brother, he changed his mind. The ex-Ranger had shown James what a lawman could do and that justice could be served. Whatever Chino had done, the Rangers could make sure he met justice face-to-face.

He damn well hoped that would happen.

"You do what you need to with Duffy and I'll get the horses ready." James busied himself checking the saddles and cinches on Bernie and Kick. Then he watered them both. By the time he was done, the women had swapped clothes.

He barely kept the words in his throat that clambered to be released at the sight before him. Cat apparently had bigger breasts than Duffy. The black clothes gaped at the buttons, showing an enticing amount of flesh. The trousers were also tight, much tighter than the baggy ones Cat usually wore. Those were now hanging on Duffy's leaner form.

Cat narrowed her gaze at him. "You say one word about my tits and I'll punch you stupid."

Duffy smothered a laugh. "We don't need to be twins. This will work from a distance." She put Cat's hat on her head. "Wrap up your hair and put on the hat. With any luck, most of the folks in the camp will follow Chino or at least be looking that direction. Move fast and don't look back."

Cat shook the other woman's hand. "The man you saw is my brother, Ben Graham. He's riding Paladin and heading west. Tell him Kitty sent you."

"You're Kitty?"

"I was a very long time ago. Now I'm Cat. Catherine Graham."

"And I'm Grace Beckett." She adjusted the hat on her head. "Duffy was my maiden name. It seemed a good choice."

"Nice to meet you, Grace." James wanted to get this over with. "Where's your horse?"

"Over yonder. I'll be on my way." She looked into Cat's eyes for a moment. "Thank you." As she walked away, Cat watched with concern.

James swung up on his gelding's back and met her gaze. "Let's go get your yearlings."

They waited at the edge of the woods for two minutes. Then Duffy, or rather Grace, exploded out of the woods. She let out a battle cry that would rival the craziest of Indian warriors. As she shot her pistol into the air, the men in the camp ran for their horses. She streaked across the ground, the horse she rode a beautiful creature with incredible lines.

"Holy shit." Cat whistled under her breath. "That woman does look like me."

James couldn't argue with her. If he didn't know it was Grace, he might have thought it was Cat.

"Nothing wrong with a woman who can ride like the wind." He squeezed her tight. "Then they can ride with you or beside you every day."

"That was almost sweet."

"I can be sweet."

She snorted, her voice unsteady. "If I wasn't scared enough to piss my britches, I might tell you that was the nicest thing you've said to me."

He had no idea what was about to happen. As the crowds followed Grace, James and Cat spurred their horses forward.

It was time.

CHAPTER FOURTEEN

Cat thought she would lose her nerve but she didn't. Oh, she was scared, more than she'd ever been in her life, but she was also determined. She would get back the yearlings and pity the man who tried to stop her.

They galloped toward the corral, arriving in less than a minute. She vaulted from the saddle and threw open the corral gate.

"Hiyah! Hiyah!" She slapped the rump of the nearest horse and then another and another. As they began to run out the open gate, she leapt onto the fence and waited until she saw Biscuit.

The sound of thundering hooves echoed through her. She whistled sharply and the yearling's ears twitched. She did it again and he moved toward her. She had hurt him and she'd hoped he would forgive her.

When he raced toward her, Cat's heart thumped. The work she did with the young horses was important. It wasn't just her job. It was who she was. To break her trust with one of them had wounded her more than it had Biscuit.

He reached her and she slid onto his back. She leaned forward to speak in his ear. "Let's go home, boy."

She whistled again and the Circle Eight yearlings moved toward her. Cat took off heading south, knowing that James, Kick and her horses were behind her. Riding bareback was second nature to her, although she would feel it later. It didn't matter. None of it mattered if they didn't keep going as fast and as hard as they could.

The last of the sun was sliding into the horizon, leaving purple shadows around them. Riding in the dark was dangerous, especially over unknown ground, but they didn't have a choice.

Ride, ride, ride.

She pushed her fear aside and let her body take over. It knew what to do and so did the horse beneath her. She'd taught them all from the moment they took their first wobbly steps. Biscuit was nearly two, the oldest of her yearlings. She should start calling him a colt. Given how well he rode with her on his back, he'd earned the new label.

"Cat!" James called from behind her.

She turned to find him on her right. He pointed and she looked back to see the yearlings spread out in a haphazard line. She'd ridden them too hard. Not all of them had the same stamina.

She patted Biscuit's neck and eased up until he slowed down. The horses all caught up to them, breathing and huffing. They needed water and a rest. There were no water sources in sight. She shouldn't have run like a madwoman.

"What have I done?"

James took off his hat. "Somehow led us away from that place and through unfamiliar woods safely."

"What?"

The horses gathered around her. She looked at each of them in turn, stupidly happy to see their beautiful faces again. Kick still had Ben's saddle on him, looking a bit lost without a rider.

"I thought maybe you knew the trail so I followed you. Are you telling me you were just riding?" James didn't sound happy about that.

"Does it matter now?" Cat didn't want to let regrets cloud the decisions they needed to make to survive.

"No, but you scare the hell out of me, woman."

She decided to take that as a compliment. "We need to find water."

"And a place to stop before it's pitch dark." His face was a blur in the murky twilight.

"Then stop jawing about it and get moving." She dismounted and went over to Kick. The ending shook his mane as she approached. "You're a smart one. Thank you for staying with us."

She mounted the gelding and started riding again, this time at a canter. The horses were safe for now. If they were lucky, Chino wouldn't be able to follow their tracks.

The men in the camp would be furious to find fifty horses missing. If anyone caught Cat and James, they'd be dead before morning. She wanted to keep moving through the night, no matter how much James protested.

They might not survive if they didn't.

The woman was driven like no other person he'd met, and that included his brother Tobias. James was falling asleep in the saddle before he finally convinced her to stop for the night.

They secured the horses near an embankment on a small creek bed. Enough grass to feed hungry equines and keep them watered.

Cat settled down on the bedroll, mentioning something about how Ben would be annoyed when he found half a bedroll on Paladin's saddle. She was asleep in minutes. James wasn't far behind. He collapsed beside her and pulled her close.

It felt like two minutes passed, but was likely hours, before she stirred in his arms. He cracked his eyes open to find she'd turned and was now facing him. In the early-morning light, the blanket had slid down to her waist. The black shirt she'd donned gaped open, several buttons undone.

His dick hardened in an instant, pushing the blood through his system. He should look away or cover her up, but he didn't. The last several days had been intense and exhausting. He needed to be near her, to remind himself they were still alive. That they should keep on fighting to survive and get back home.

Home was another topic he wasn't ready to think about. Going back to the livery after this seemed wrong, like a shirt that didn't fit. Sort of like the shirt Cat had on. It worked but it wouldn't last long.

James didn't want to think about what would happen in a couple more days, when he'd have to face life again. His hand still ached from the knife cut, the one thing that reminded him he'd started this adventure because he was convenient. Whoever the first person was to show up at the Circle Eight would have been roped into helping Cat.

It happened to be James. And it happened to change his life

forever. Sometimes he grew angry at life, for throwing challenges, tragedies and losses in his path. This time, however, it had thrown Catherine Frances Graham.

A gift he would never understand. He wouldn't have thought himself the kind of man to fall for a woman. He'd fallen hard enough to make him question everything he'd thought was important.

James stared at her face, at the smudge of dirt on her cheek and the snarls in her hair. She wasn't perfect, but she was perfect for him.

Her eyes popped open. "What are you doing?"

He refused to be embarrassed for looking at the woman he loved. "Watching you sleep."

"That's strange."

"Not really. You are busier than a hive of bees when you're awake." He traced her cheek with one finger. "It's the only time you're still enough to look at you."

She wrinkled her nose. "I'm not sure if that's a compliment or not."

He smiled. "Would I insult you?"

"You have."

"Unfair."

"So is being told you're unimportant because you're female."

He winced. "Did I do that?"

"You did. And I wanted to kick you in the balls."

He resisted the urge to cup said balls. "I suppose I deserved it."

"I thought so, but Hannah talked me out of it."

"Remind me to thank her. My balls should thank her too."

Cat laughed softly. "How did I not see who you were?"

"I didn't see you either." He leaned forward and kissed her. "I see you now."

Her lips opened under his, and he dove into the warm recesses of her mouth. She moaned and sucked at his tongue, making his dick twitch.

"We shouldn't do this." Her voice was breathy and unsteady.

"Mmmm, no we shouldn't." He kissed his way down her jaw to neck. He busied himself unbuttoning the rest of her shirt, releasing those marvelous breasts.

She arched her back, providing him free access. He pulled a nipple into his mouth, the turgid peak tightening on his tongue. His pulse throbbed right along with every muscle in his body. She was like heaven in his arms, soft and feminine.

He slid his hand down her belly to the trousers. "These are still on."

"You haven't taken them off."

He tugged at the buttons but they held fast. "I might need help."

She smacked his shoulder. "Keep licking my tits. I like that."

"Yes, ma'am." He held fast to her nipple, sometimes biting them, as she wiggled her way out of the trousers that belonged to Duffy, or rather, to Grace.

"Your teeth feel so good." She pulled his hand between her legs. "Do it again while you touch my pussy."

He would have to get used to her plain talking. Although he wouldn't mind hearing it. Truth was, it excited him. He liked hearing the words "tits" and "pussy" coming from her.

As his fingers slid into her folds, she sucked in a breath. "Yessss."

He nibbled, laved and suckled at her nipple, then the other. Her skin had a sheen of perspiration as she moved against his hand. Her sweet heat surrounded him.

"I need more, James. More." She grabbed at his trousers. "Please."

Who was he to turn her down? He wasn't sure if he could actually get the damn trousers off given how hard his dick was. Somehow he managed it though, tossing them in a pile with hers. She lay on her side watching him, her hand between her legs and the other pinching her nipple. The woman knew no boundaries. She was pleasuring herself in front of him.

James thought he was aroused before. He was so very wrong. "Jesus, Cat, you're going to make me come before I get near you."

She smiled, one he expected every woman since the beginning of time had bestowed on her man. "Touch yourself. I want to see."

He grabbed the base of his dick and squeezed. She got to her knees, her hand still moving on her pussy and moved closer. Her mouth was inches from him as he slid his hand up and down, tugging and squeezing his staff.

"Does it feel good?"

"Not as good as your pussy."

Her eyes widened. "Can I lick it?"

He groaned. "God, yes."

She reached out and gave a tentative lick with her tongue. He held his breath. Her hot mouth closed over the head and he almost fell over. Every ounce of blood went to his cock, pulsing and throbbing in her mouth. She was inexperienced, but a quick learner.

When her mouth slid down to where his hand held the base of his staff. Her warm lips touched his fingers and he shuddered, his balls tight with need.

"I don't want to come in your mouth."

She murmured something he couldn't hear, but her hand moved faster between her legs.

"Let me put this inside you, honey. We'll both feel good." As he pulled his cock from her mouth, he wanted to put it back into the most beautiful lips in the world.

"Can we do this again?" She wiped her mouth with the back of her hand.

"Anytime you want. Now lay back."

She shook her head. "Nope. You lay back."

He raised his brows but obeyed. There was no way he would turn down her riding him. Ever.

As she rose over him, she spread her legs and guided his staff into her scorching heat. "I've been listening to stories for years from my sisters, now it's my turn to experience it."

He didn't want to think about her family or anything else. "Hush up and ride me, Catherine."

As she sank onto his length, her eyes closed and her head went back. He cupped her breasts, pinching the already red nipples. She started moving up and down, slowly at first. Then she found a rhythm and picked up speed.

"When I move down onto you, it hits my pussy hard and feels so good." She moved with grace, an exquisite creature who swayed above him, pulling him toward a powerful orgasm.

"It feels good to me too. So damn good." He gripped her hips, guiding her faster and faster.

Her breath came in choppy bursts. He thrust up into her as she pushed down. His balls tightened to near pain and then suddenly he was falling into a maelstrom of pleasure. Ecstasy exploded through him. He whispered her name as she tightened around him, milking his cock while her muscles fluttered and pulsed.

Cat collapsed onto him while he was still embedded within her. He stroked her back, glad they'd taken a chance and made love. He kissed her shoulder and closed his eyes.

To have a moment of perfection in the midst of a storm of fear and evil was a gift. Catherine was a gift.

Sometime later, they lay face-to-face, mostly naked, their bodies cooling in the dawn air. James was ridiculously calm after making love to her. He rolled over and found their clothes, then tried to help her button the too-small shirt.

"I don't think it's going to fit no matter what you do."

"It's these marvelous breasts." He cupped them again. "I can't top touching them."

"You're tit-obsessed, aren't you?" Before he could respond, she jerked forward, almost knocking her head into his. "What the hell was that?" Cat peered behind her. "Damn horse. Which one of you—" She gasped so loud, he reached for his gun.

"What?"

"Sparrow?" She got to her feet, tripping over the bedroll. "Holy shit. Holy shit. Holy shit. James." She turned to him. "The mares and foals. They found us."

James stood and peered at the figures behind Cat. Somehow the rest of the Circle Eight horses had tracked them to the hidden creek bed. He would've never believed it if he hadn't seen it. One of the foals pranced around its dam, his ears twitching.

"This is Starling's sister." Cat petted the mare. "She had her first foal last year. Chester hasn't stopped moving since." Her voice was thick with emotion as she embraced the small horse.

"Do you name all your females after birds?" He hadn't realized it until just then. He supposed he should have asked her about the horses before now. It was an integral part of who she was. If he loved her, he should know all there was about that which she loved so much.

"My mother used to point out all the birds to us. Taught us the bird songs and we had games to guess the bird before anyone else." Cat returned her attention to the rest of the horses that had appeared in their makeshift camp. "I hear her voice every time I bring a filly into the world."

James looked around. There were two of them and nearly two dozen horses. How were they going to manage herding them alone? He knew they were well trained and they all responded to Cat, but he didn't know what to do. Their plan had only included the yearlings. Now they had twice as many horses to manage.

He wasn't the type of man to admit readily if he needed help. Ever. Yet if they were to find a way to get back safely, he was going to have to ask her how.

His pride was a hard thing to swallow.

"What do we do with all them?" He was surprised to find his voice steady and sure.

"We take them home."

"How? I've never handled more than half a dozen horses at once. Most of these don't have lead ropes or bridles, much less reins."

"They got here on their own by following me. I've trained them all with whistles." She met his gaze. "If we can stay low and out of sight, I can get them home. Trust me."

"I trust you." He could hear the truth in his voice and his heart echoed the sentiment. A welcome shock to know he had found someone in whom to place his trust.

"I think this is the creek that runs around the edge of the MacRae's ranch. We follow it, the horses stay watered and fed. It will take us an extra day since we can't ride hard, but it's our safest route." Her expression was confident and sure.

He wished he didn't want to grab her and ride like hell for home. It was selfish and he knew that, but he couldn't erase the thought.

"I'm worried we won't make it with all these horses." He spoke low even though the damn animals couldn't understand him. "We can ride like hell and get home more quickly."

She sighed. "You're right. You head back to the Circle Eight and draw away anybody following us. I'll take the horses through the creek like we planned."

He stared at her. "Hell and damnation, Cat, do you think I'd abandon you?"

"No, but maybe if they're following you, they won't follow me."

He yanked her against him and hugged her so hard their hearts beat in unison. "If you'd told me that a week ago I would've listened to you. Not now."

"Not now," she repeated.

"No. I can't begin to tell you how much I don't want to be separated from you." James thought maybe he sounded like a lovesick calf.

"Neither do I. When did I get so attached to you?" She punched his arm. "I think we need to go back to not liking each other."

"Too late."

She leaned back and kissed him, her lips soft as a flower petal. He breathed in her scent, pulling her deep into his body. She'd become part of who he was. He couldn't lose her now.

"We have to try."

He squeezed her hands. "Yep, we do. Let's show them what the Grahams and Gibsons are made of."

She smiled and his heart stuttered at the sight. "Damn right."

James knew whatever happened, they couldn't go back to where they were before the horses were stolen. What the future held was a mystery. All they had was here and now. This woman was everything to him.

He would fight for what they had, what they could have.

CHAPTER FIFTEEN

Cat was a little tender between her legs but it was a good discomfort. Each time she twinged, she remembered why and smiled to herself. Their situation was dangerous, but they'd taken the time to make love. She was glad of it. What if they didn't make it back home alive? She didn't want to go to her death without taking a chance to be with the man she loved.

Every moment she was with him solidified the emotion she had identified as love. Her sisters and sisters-in-law had tried to explain it to her, but it was only when she acknowledged her feelings that she understood it fully.

Now she couldn't imagine being the person she was when she left the Circle Eight. Coming home would feel odd knowing James wasn't there with her. Cat didn't expect to marry but if he asked her, she knew she would say yes. In fact, if he didn't ask her, she would do the honors.

Why not? Cat had never been traditional. She wouldn't let something like what she should do stand in her way. As she led the horses through the creek toward home, they followed her two-by-two. She was thankful to have trained them with her various whistles. The foals didn't yet respond to her. They frolicked along, exploring the creek bed, never straying more than a few feet away from their dams.

If they weren't running for their lives, it would have been peaceful.

She kept her gaze moving from side by side. They were mostly hidden from anyone riding past by the trees and the sunken creek bed. That didn't mean someone wouldn't hear a herd of two dozen horses splashing through water.

James rode at the end of their parade while she led the way.

The hours passed with grueling slowness. The horses had to pick their way through the rocky and sometimes sandy bottom of the creek. In parts where the bank was wide enough, they stayed in the grassy areas. However, their pace never moved past a walk. The foals weren't big enough and they were still exhausted from the mad dash from the Circle Eight.

Hell, she was exhausted. Beyond that though. It seemed to be a weak word for how she felt. If she got home, Cat might sleep for a week. She stopped herself from continuing. It wasn't "if", it was "when" she returned to the Circle Eight.

They had little food, so they ate smaller portions, supplementing with berries when they found them. James's whiskers had grown into a beard after not shaving for four days. It lent him a sinister darkness that she knew was false. Beneath that fierce man lay a heart of gold.

When they stopped for the night, the moon was high in the sky and night had fallen many hours earlier. To her surprise, they hadn't heard anyone riding nearby. A few herds of cattle lowing and other animals such as deer and foxes. No humans however. That was what pushed her to keep going even when she was afraid she would fall off Kick's back.

She groaned when her feet hit the spongy ground. James appeared beside her, touching her elbow.

"You've got grit, woman. I'll give you that."

She managed a wobbly smile. "Sheer stubbornness."

He snorted. "I can believe that."

She swatted his arm. "We're a matched pair for that. You still don't even like me."

He pulled her close. "Not true, Catherine. Not true at all." He kissed her softly and then held her.

Her eyes burned with unshed tears. They were so far from home. By her estimate, at the pace they were moving, it would be another two days to reach the Circle Eight. Two days of anxiety and danger. She wasn't sure she would make it without the man who wrapped his arms around her.

He rubbed her back. The soft sounds of the horses settling in for the night mixed with the song from the night peepers and frogs. It was peaceful, or at least as much as it could be considering the circumstances. She sighed against his shoulder. "Thank you."

His hand stopped. "Did you just thank me?"

She barked a laugh. "I promise I'm not that bad."

"You're welcome." His hand moved again and she closed her eyes, nearly lulled to sleep while still on her feet. "Let's eat and get some shuteye while we can."

As had become their habit, they laid out equal portions of food. Cat plucked the last two peach halves from the jar and smiled. Eva had given them both a taste of home without being with them.

"What is your obsession with peaches?" James asked as he accepted the plate from her.

Cat grinned. "It's my favorite treat. Eva always used them as a bribe." Too many memories of home crowded her mind. "I miss my family."

"Me too." He slipped the peach onto her plate.

"Why did you do that?" She stared at the sweet treat. "Nobody gives up a peach from Eva."

"I'd give up my life for you, Catherine." His dark gaze was intense in the moonlight. "Why not a peach?"

Her throat had tightened and she couldn't get a word out, much less a bite down. It had been the sweetest thing anyone in her life had said to her. Her love for James grew deeper with every moment that passed.

She didn't protest when he laid out one bedroll between a few trees away from the damp ground by the creek. He lay down and she joined him, spooning against him beneath the blanket.

Cat didn't know how long she slept before she woke with a start. Her heart pounded and she didn't know why. She strained to hear anything beyond the thumping in her chest and the whooshing sound of the blood rushing past her ears.

"What's wrong?" James whispered.

"Listen," was all she said.

They were both silent for a minute. Then Cat understood what she heard, or rather, what she didn't hear. The insects and frogs were silent.

One of the horses whinnied, then another. Cat jumped to her feet, pistol in hand. James was right beside her.

"Something's out there." She felt the horses' alarm. They were bumping into each other and making sounds of distress. The foals sounded as though they cried for their mamas, a high-pitched bleat followed by the dams' whinny.

"It's not human." James sniffed the air. "Coyote or mountain lion."

Every Texan had battled the elements, the predators and the weather. With so many horses to protect in pitch darkness, Cat and James were at a distinct disadvantage. Whatever was out there could pick off one of the babies with ease.

She gripped the pistol and wished like hell they'd built a fire before going to sleep. Regrets wouldn't help now. Action would. She called on every bit of her knowledge from her family.

"I'm going to put out jerky to lure it." She dug into the saddlebags beside the bedroll. "You circle around to the left. I'll go right. If we're lucky the little fucker will go after the easy meat first."

She left the three strips they had remaining on the rock nearby. The horses milled around, scared and confused. She whistled low and soft to ease their fears. If they didn't calm down, she and James would never find the predator in time.

She crept around, patting the horses and whistling under her breath. A low growl sounded from behind her. She whirled around, gun cocked and readied herself for a fight.

Nothing.

Cat moved back from where she came. Her heart was about to crack a rib it beat so damn hard. She reached Kick and he shoved his head into her side. She bit back an angry shout. The horses were all scared. He was just letting her know it.

Another growl from in front of her. She crept close and saw a shadow move. Cat aimed and waited for it to move again. Her hand was steady and her anger pushing aside the cold fear. She hadn't gone through all of this just to lose her horses to a hungry predator.

When the shadow rushed toward her, she squeezed the trigger even as another shot rang out. A body slid toward her on the ground with a yip and a grunt. Dirt rose up in a cloud as it came to a stop. The acrid scent of gunpowder mixed with the coppery smell of blood.

"Cat?"

She managed to swallow the lump in her throat. "I'm here."

"I think I got it."

She scoffed. "No, I got it."

He appeared beside her, his body warmth evident in the cool night air. She wanted to crawl back into his arms, but that wasn't what they should do and she knew it.

"Coyote." He pushed at the body before them. "We can't stay here."

"I know. The blood will bring his friends, or worse." She squeezed his hand and released it quickly. Much as she wanted to crawl back beneath the blanket and settle in his arms, they needed to move fast.

He grabbed her and kissed her hard. "Time to ride."

They rode through the rest of the night, stopping to rest for half an hour before moving on. By the time the sun was high in the sky, James forgot what sleep was. He moved forward using pure fear for Cat. Nothing could happen to her, no matter what. He would keep her safe. James called on his inner beast to protect his mate. The coyote inside him had embraced his protective instincts and bared its teeth.

James couldn't let his guard down for a minute. It was the mare Sparrow who alerted him to the danger. He'd been riding behind the merry line of horses, watching the foals as they explored with childish curiosity. Sparrow, sister to the fallen Starling, perked her ears and whinnied for her baby. The little one listened, returning to his dam, keeping within inches of her powerful forelegs.

James knew a lot about horses, even before he co-owned a livery with his brother. They smelled danger long before humans did. James heard the hooves before he saw anything.

He whistled high like Cat had taught him to. All the horses stopped. Cat stood up in the stirrups and looked back at him. He pointed to the right and she whipped her head around to peer through the trees.

It was a group of horses coming straight toward their escape route where they were hidden from view. There was nothing they could do except be as quiet as possible. Hard to do with so many equines, but to his surprise, they stood on alert, their ears moving and listening.

The intruders grew closer and closer. If they came to the edge of the embankment, the strangers would see them below. James ground his teeth and slipped the gun from its holster. The rifle wasn't far behind. He wouldn't be taken without a fight.

The horses stopped perhaps twenty feet from the embankment that led to the creek. To his surprise, Cat had crawled up on Kick's saddle. She crouched with her pistol in one hand, a rifle in the other. The black hat was missing, likely because it wasn't hers and it blocked her view.

Time slowed as they waited in excruciating silence. James heard murmurs of conversation. He held his breath waiting for the group to ride away. They didn't sound as if they were looking for anyone.

"Jeb and Katie, I know you're in there." Chino's voice smashed the silence into sharp shards that slammed into James.

Fuck.

"I followed you for a while then I lost you. Took me a day to figure out what you were doing." Chino chuffed a laugh. "I knew I couldn't trust you. As soon as my back is turned, you steal my fucking horses."

Cat growled. He couldn't see her expression, but James knew she was ready to fight to the death for *her* horses.

"If you come out now and return them, I'll let you go free."

James didn't believe that for a minute. Chino didn't even sound as if he was trying to be truthful.

"Or I'll kill you and likely kill a few of them. You cost me money by taking my damn horses and I'll make sure you pay before you die. Don't doubt I won't fuck you to death, *chica*." Chino's menace had returned, and with it, James's fury.

How dare that bastard threaten Cat? The thieving jackass had already cost the Grahams plenty.

"Your friend who killed my buyer, I'm going to find him after I finish with you two." Chino paused. "Lots of pain and death or go free without the horses. You got one minute to decide."

James knew without asking that Cat didn't want to risk the horses' lives. But she also knew Chino was lying. They had little choice but to surrender.

She stood up in the saddle, her face flushed with fury. "You fucking *stole* those horses. They don't belong to you."

"That's where you're wrong, *chica*. They're mine." Chino appeared at the top of the embankment, his clothes dusted with dirt and sweat. "Bring them up here and I won't kill you. Last chance."

Cat's grip tightened on the pistol and James thought for a moment she would shoot the man through the head. However the shadows of the men behind her must've stayed her hand. James didn't lower his own pistol until she tucked hers back into its holster.

She sat back down on Kick's saddle and climbed the embankment. The horses followed her. They reached the open prairie to find Chino's gang waiting. Whitey and Al were expressionless while Red looked as angry as his boss.

Cat's rage, however, put them all to shame. No longer playing the part of Katie, she thrust her shoulders back and threw herself from the saddle. As she stalked toward Chino, she was magnificent. A woman as strong, smart and brave as any man who walked the Earth.

He'd thought he loved her before. It wasn't until this moment he recognized the depth of his feelings for her. It wasn't temporary. It wouldn't fade away when they returned to their lives, *if* they returned. No, he loved her to the center of his soul, embedded deep in in his bones.

Forever.

James jumped down from his horse and joined her. Chino crossed his arms and widened his stance. Cat got right up in his face, her face contorted with fury.

"You are so evil, the depths of hell would spit you back out. You steal and murder to line your pockets. What kind of man does that?" Her words echoed through the air.

James was almost amused to see Al and Whitey step back a few feet. He didn't blame them. She was frightening in her anger and vengeance.

"I'll tell you what kind of man. A coward. A yellow-bellied coward who can't be a real man so he takes what doesn't belong to him. A thief. Something to scrape off my bottom of my shit-covered boot."

To everyone's shock, she pulled her fist back and punched Chino so hard, he stumbled backward. She jumped on him, but Red grabbed her and threw her to the right. James roared and punched the son of a bitch. Nobody hurt his woman.

Chino regained his balance and pulled his pistol. As the barrel moved toward Cat, time seemed to stop. A bullet would not end the amazing creature that was Catherine Frances Graham. James wouldn't let that happen.

He pushed at her shoulders, moving between her and Chino. It wasn't heroic. It was what James had to do. There was little in his life he could call the right thing, but this was one of them.

When the gunshot sounded, he landed atop Cat, the breath knocked from his body. Yet there was no pain, no blood. He looked down at her scowling, reddened face.

"Get off me, Gibson. I can't breathe."

He didn't feel insulted she hadn't appreciated saving her. At least that's what he told himself.

James got to his knees and she sat up immediately. "What were you thinking? You could've been killed."

"I was trying to save your life."

"Don't you know by now that I can save myself?"

"Why can't you let me be the man? I've got a dick and you well know it."

"I'm gonna have to stop this right here." Matt Graham's voice cut through their argument.

Cat's mouth dropped open at whoever stood behind James, which definitely included her oldest brother. He was almost afraid to look.

Cat's emotions took over her at the sight of her brothers and her brother-in-law. A fierce wall of muscle and gun pointed straight at Chino and his three cohorts. Matt, Caleb, Nick and Brody, along with another tall, thin man with graying red hair stood in a semi-circle. Her brothers had varying shades of brown hair, blue-green eyes, wide shoulders and the Graham ferocity in their veins.

Her brother-in-law, Brody, was another man who wore black most of the time. His bright blue eyes were the only pop of color in his dark countenance. He'd married her oldest sister, Olivia, after retiring from the Texas Rangers. Now a farmer, he still liked to ride into danger now and again.

"I see you found the horses, Cat." Matt's voice was colder than the steel in his hand.

"These are the thieves who stole them." Cat scrambled to her feet. She pointed at Chino. "He's responsible for Starling's death."

"You slit her throat, you dumb bitch," Red spoke up.

Cat didn't even see James move, but suddenly he was standing over Red, his hand fisted and the other man out cold in the dirt.

"Nobody talks to her like that." He looked at Chino, Al and Whitey. "Anybody else?"

"I guess you were in good hands, little sister." Matt turned his attention to Chino, who sneered at her.

"I knew you were one of them cocky Grahams. You can't hide your nature."

"Damn right I am. And I've got tits too. The woman, the *Graham*, who stole her horses back from under your nose." She'd had enough of the thief's mouth.

"I'd like to start with the arresting now." The stranger with red hair glanced at Caleb. "These are your missing horses, right?"

"That they are, Rooster." Matt gestured to Chino. "And I'm wondering why this piece of shit took them."

As the eldest Graham who had to become the patriarch of the family when he was only twenty-three, Matt had seen too many dark things in his life to not expect the worst of people. He was tough, protective and sometimes annoying, but she had never been so glad to see him.

To her horror, tears rolled down her face. She tried to swipe them away, but Nick spotted them. His eyes widened.

"Are you crying?" He couldn't have asked any louder. Damn him.

Matt glanced at her in surprise. He frowned. "Cat?"

She shook her head, too emotional to speak. When he opened his arms, she flew into them. He took a few steps back, holding her while she sobbed like she had when she'd been a little girl.

"Chino and these three stole the horses. We tracked them,

found Starling's foal and had to bury the poor thing. We caught up with them and pretended to hire up." James put his hands on his hips. "Catherine had to put Starling down, then we rode into a camp about a day's ride from here. Chino had a regular buyer who paid him to steal horses. He's killed folks too."

"Why steal the young ones and the mares?" Caleb seemed angrier than any of them, which surprised her. It had been Nick who was mad at the world, but married life had calmed him down considerably. If she wasn't crying like an idiot, she might have smiled at the thought.

"It was what he was paid to do. The buyer targeted the Circle Eight." James's voice was laced with fury. "He wanted to hurt the Grahams. I don't think it was about the money. It was personal."

Matt patted her shoulder. "What say you, Cat?"

She looked up at him through teary eyes. "James is right. The man knew the Grahams. I was never so glad to not have your eye color."

"I knewed you was a Graham."

"Shut up." James growled at Chino.

"What was the buyer's name?" Brody asked.

"Manfred Cunningham."

The silence that followed the name was scarier than facing down Chino's pistol. Cat stepped away from her brother and swiped her eyes with her sleeves.

"What is it?"

"Are you sure that was his name?" Caleb sounded deadly furious.

"I'm sure." She would never forget it.

Caleb looked to the man named Rooster. "You arrest these fools. I'm going after Cunningham." He turned to his horse.

"He's dead." Cat's words stopped him in his tracks.

"You sure?"

She would have trouble blocking the image of his death from her memories. "I'm sure. Ben killed him."

Caleb closed his eyes. Matt let loose a string of curses that would have made any normal female blush.

"Where is he?" Matt took her by the shoulders.

"He took Paladin and ran. Said he couldn't go to prison. I

didn't know what to do." Her eyes filled with tears again. "It was like he was dead inside. He told us what the man did to him."

While Rooster cuffed the four thieves with Brody's help, Matt, Caleb and Nick stood around her, their expressions a mixture of worry and frustration.

"What did he say?" Matt's voice had gentled.

James stepped up beside her, saving her from repeating the awful truth. "He said Cunningham had been the one to train him to please Pablo, the man who'd bought him. Manfred had kept him for a year because Ben was his favorite."

"Fuck. If he wasn't dead, I'd cut him into pieces, then light them on fire." Caleb vibrated with rage. "Pablo Garza's real name was Cunningham too. His brother no doubt."

Cat felt sick to her stomach. Brothers stealing little boys for awful things. Ben would never be the same, if they ever saw him again. She remembered the emptiness of his eyes, the way he hadn't cared about his ravaged hands, and the finality of his decision. He was lost to her, and her heart finally wept for the loss.

Matt cupped her cheek. "You did the right thing, little one."

Her chin rumbled and she'd never felt so young or weak. If only she could have stopped Ben. If only she could have saved Starling. She could wallpaper her life with regrets and "if onlys".

In the end, her brother was gone, one horse and her foal were dead, and she would never, ever be the same.

"Let's go home."

CHAPTER SIXTEEN

James rode with the Graham siblings toward the Circle Eight. Their interactions didn't surprise him any longer. He'd watched them before and during the wedding between his brother Tobias and their sister Rebecca last fall. They were close enough to tease each other and two minutes later, yell at each other.

Envy over their closeness wormed its way into his heart again. He wanted that with Tobias, more than he ever thought it would. He just didn't know how to make that happen. The Grahams had once again bonded over Ben's crime and subsequent flight. All of them sick with worry over their little brother.

Then there was the fact he was kept separated from Cat. Intentionally, he was sure. If one brother wasn't there, another was. After her scary brother-in-law disappeared with the Ranger named Rooster and the prisoners, the three Graham brothers decided to put themselves bodily between he and Cat.

After the first few times, he could have dismissed it. Then he recognized it for what it was. They were protecting their baby sister.

Damn it.

He needed to talk to her. What he'd say, he had no idea, but he knew he couldn't get back to the Circle Eight without saying what his heart told him to. James figured whatever it needed to say, he'd figure it out. If only he got the chance to do more than see her ass end on a horse.

Matt put him on drag again, but this time he resented it because her three brothers and twenty horses were between them. And there was no doubt in his mind he would *not* be spooning

Cat that night.

Time slipped through his fingers as they rode more efficiently across the dry ground. With five armed riders, they were less likely to run into any trouble. No matter who from the camp might also be chasing them, Chino and his cohorts were safely in the hands of the Texas Rangers.

There was nothing left to do but get the horses back home. If only that didn't sound like a door closing in James's face. He helped out, chased a couple of the yearlings who decided to race each other, built a fire, doused the fire, made coffee and stared at Cat.

Caleb growled at him. Matt scowled. Nick gave him the stink eye. It was ridiculous and annoying. Cat was a grown woman who could make her own choices.

Yet she avoided his gaze. He told himself she was tired and overcome, but it was a lie. It was the middle of the night and he hadn't slept a wink. The cold bedroll was no substitute for a warm woman. A woman he loved desperately.

He got to his feet and headed for the small pond he'd seen earlier. Perhaps a midnight swim would cool the annoyance and frustration coursing through his veins.

The frogs were singing loud and proud in the night. He pulled off his clothes and waded into the water. He flipped on his back and floated for a while, letting the ripples steer his body.

"You know this reminds me of the night I tried to wash up in the creek and you pleasured me." Cat's voice floated across the night air.

He started and got to his feet, slicking his hair back. She stood on the bank of the pond, the moonlight shining down on her, turning her into an ethereal being, a fairy in the woods. She was exquisite.

He shook his head to dispel the fanciful thoughts. Now wasn't the time to let his heart overrule his good sense. "Do your brothers know you're here?"

"Of course not. They tend to frown on me and naked men." She sat on a fallen log, wrapping her arms around her legs.

"If I remember it right, you were naked." He gestured to the water, his dick already rising to the possibility of being with Cat. "Join me?"

She chuckled. "You know I can't. If they find us, you won't back it back to Briar Creek."

"Hell, if they find us with *me* naked, they'll shoot my balls off." He sincerely hoped that didn't happen. He was fond of his balls.

"That's why I'm going to sit here even if I want to dive in there and kiss you so hard I ache from it."

His heart stopped for a few moments, then it kicked into high gear, sending every drop of blood between his legs. James was lightheaded and harder than an oak tree.

God he wanted her.

"I wanted to thank you."

He shook his head to clear the thought of kissing her. "Thank me for what?"

"For being with me during this whole thing. I know you didn't even want to come. You did it because Eva made you promise you would." She sighed. "I don't know how this would've ended if you hadn't been by my side."

He shrugged off the thanks, unwilling to contemplate an ending where Cat would've ended up dead and alone.

"I never expected to like you. Especially after you kissed me last year." She got to her feet. "I never knew what love was. Not really. I never knew what fear was either. Not the deep kind. I'm not sure what will happen tomorrow when we get back to the Circle Eight, but I wanted to thank you."

"You said that." His ardor began to wane with each "thank you".

"I wanted to make sure you heard it."

"I heard it. You can go back to sleep now." He dove into the water, swimming away from her, from the heartbreak she was about to inflict on him. James was smart enough to hear it coming.

"You're still a jackass." She disappeared into the night, leaving him to wonder if he'd ever recover from loving Catherine Frances Graham.

Cat couldn't sleep after she returned to her own bed. The ranch felt different even though it wasn't. Yes, Paladin and her favorite mare were gone, but the yearlings were back where they belonged, as were the mares and the foals. She'd eaten her fill of Maria's cooking until she thought her stomach might pop.

Yet Cat couldn't sleep. The hours crawled by until she finally gave up. She'd only been home for eight hours but she was already regretting it. How could a week with James change everything in her life?

She loved him, that was certain, but when she tried to tell him, she'd made a mess of things. Ended up thanking him numerous times, which apparently stung his pride.

Every time she closed her eyes, she saw his face as he said goodbye to her earlier in the day. He'd refused Eva's cooking and brushed aside her thanks for bringing her *hija* home safe. To Cat, he appeared to run back to town, to his life, away from her. As fast as he could.

She pulled on her clothes and walked out to the barn, not bothering to light a lamp. The path was so familiar, she only needed her memory to guide her. She stepped into the barn and breathed in the scents. This was home, not the house or her bed. The horse barn was where she belonged. She made the decision right then to tell Matt she was moving into the old bunks Javier and Lorenzo used to live in.

It might be odd and lonely but that's what she wanted. The house didn't fit any longer. Her discomfort might be due to her adventure with James, but she attributed it more to what she'd witnessed while she was away from home.

She closed the door behind her and walked to Sparrow's stall. Perhaps she wanted to be near the closest horse to Starling. Her guilt might not ever abate over what she'd done, no matter that the horse was in pain and dying in agony. Cat would never get over killing the mare she'd brought into the world five years earlier.

Even thinking about the death made her heart ache so hard she had to stop and lean against the wall for a moment. She pressed her fist to her chest and swallowed the tears that threatened. There was no shame in grieving for something she loved. What she was ashamed of was her part in Starling's death.

She reached Sparrow's stall and stepped in. The mare pushed her head into Cat's belly. Little Chester got to his feet, excited to have a visitor. His mother pushed him back to the corner as if telling him to go back to sleep.

"Hey, girl. I know I woke you up. I'm sorry for that. I'm sorry for a lot of things." She petted the horse's neck. "I miss her and I'm sure you do too."

Paladin and Starling both gone. Two of her favorite equines. It was hard to say goodbye to them. No matter that the horses were there to work for the humans. They were animals with hearts. She knew they loved her as much as she loved them. Cat had fresh scars on her heart for their loss.

Just being with Sparrow calmed her anxiety. Cat settled in beside Chester and snuggled the foal. The little critter lent his body heat to her and she found herself drifting off to sleep.

James missed her. Missed her so much he was distracted and made stupid mistakes. He sucked at the cut on his thumb and cursed himself. If he wasn't thinking about her, he was remembering how she tasted, how her body fit to his as though she was made for him.

He'd been repairing a stall door and the hammer slipped. He wouldn't go see Rebecca or she'd start to think he was a clumsy idiot. Considering how much he'd injured himself in the last week, he very well could be the clumsiest person in Briar Creek.

He was definitely an idiot though.

He'd left Cat at the Circle Eight with barely a goodbye. She had been hurt by his leaving. She wasn't one to hold back words, but she'd been mute when he tipped his hat and ridden away. Her eyes told him the whole story though.

Stupid. Stupid. Stupid.

A week had passed with excruciating slowness. Every hour turned into minutes and seconds, crawling past. No matter what he did, his mind drifted to Catherine Graham.

"Damn." He threw the hammer against the wood and sank to his knees. Would he never have peace again?

"I'd say you have a problem." Tobias watched from a few feet away, his expression concerned. Thank God it wasn't pity or James would have to punch him.

"Fucking right I do." James ran his hand down his face. "I'm an idiot."

"I could've told you that." Tobias snorted. "Hell, I think I *did* tell you that years ago."

James glanced at his brother. "I'm not playing anymore, Tobias. I don't know how to fix this."

His brother slid down next to him and propped up his knee. "Tell me."

This was the closeness James had craved. The relationship he had wanted with his brothers as the Grahams had with each other. It was ironic that his problem with one particular Graham would be the thing that brought he and Tobias closer together.

"Something happened while you were out chasing those horses, didn't it?"

James nodded with a jerk. "Something happened. I did something really stupid."

Tobias narrowed his gaze. "You fell in love, didn't you?"

At that, James let loose a half-sob, half-laugh. "I fell in love last year. I just didn't realize it until last week."

"Love has a way of sneaking up on you. Took me five damn years to accept it. I almost lost her for good. I'm blessed to have a woman who saw beneath the dirt and whiskey to see me." Tobias had struggled with alcohol and had pulled himself out of the bottle to remake himself. His wife, Rebecca, had become his other half. James had never seen two people so devoted to each other.

Given their history with their mother it was amazing. She'd thrown them away, went through men as though they were dishes to be consumed and forgotten, and had never given them the love a mother should.

"You're a lucky man." James envied Tobias with a sharpness he hadn't expected.

"I had to work for it. If you love her, then why the hell are you moping around the livery?"

"I told her I loved her. She thanked me for helping her." James made a face. "As if I was a temporary distraction to help her get her horses back."

"Do you really think that's what she meant? Catherine Graham doesn't strike me as someone who keeps her thoughts to herself." Tobias had a point.

"It was an intense five days, but the feelings started a year ago when I went to the Circle Eight to get Rebecca for Will. Cat followed me around, drove me crazy." He shook his head. "Then she kissed me."

Tobias nodded. "That might knock a man backwards a bit."

"Like I never had happen before. And she isn't afraid to tell me everything on her mind." James didn't know how to process what came out of her mouth.

"She is a plain-talking female."

"You have no idea how true that is. She told me what she liked with, ah, words ladies don't use."

That perked Tobias's interest. "Like what?"

"I'm not telling you. It's private between the two of us."

"Not if you aren't going to marry the girl. She'll do that with another man and you'll be a memory of five days running with her. She might even try to forget about you completely." Tobias was being deliberately cruel and it made James want to punch him.

"You don't have to be such an ass."

"If I remember correctly, you handed my ass to me several times when I was stuck in the whiskey bottle." Tobias waited for James to contradict him, but he didn't.

It was true, damn it.

"Is that what you're doing to me?"

"You've been lost since you got back. Even Will noticed. Told me you make him sad." Tobias wasn't usually the brother who made sense. Married life had changed him.

"I don't mean to." James blew out a frustrated breath. "Love hurts like hell."

"There's one way to make it stop hurting."

"You want me to go talk to her."

"No, I think you want to go talk to her. Just got to get off your ass and do it." Tobias was right again.

"What if she tells me to go to hell?" James hadn't wanted to voice his worst fear aloud, but there it was. "What if it's one-sided and I was just a distraction?"

"Then you'll know for sure." Tobias stared at him, his expression sympathetic. "All I know is if you don't talk to her, you'll *never* know."

Tobias got to his feet and brushed off the back of his trousers. "No matter what, I'm here if you need me."

He left James alone with his thoughts. The rest of the afternoon passed as he contemplated throwing himself at her feet. Cat was just as stubborn as James was. One of them had to give, but was he ready to be that person?

"Jeb?" Will poked his head in the livery door, his brows furrowed. The youngest Gibson had suffered a blow to the head by a tree, right in front of James, a year earlier. Instead of killing him, it left him with the mind of a child. He used childish nicknames, had the purest view of life and had brought Tobias and James together as a family again. He'd saved both of them.

Amazing that a tragedy could become a miracle.

"Hey, Will." James smiled in earnest at his little brother. "Done for the day?"

"I lost another checkers game to Mr. Waldeck." Will scratched at the scar that stood out above his ear where the hair never grew.

"Maybe you'll beat him tomorrow." James hung up the tools he'd been using on their pegs. "Do you want ham for supper?"

"Yes. I mean no." Will shuffled his feet. "I heard you talking with Toby. You love Miss Cat, don't you?"

Still smart as a whip.

"Yep, I do. Does that bother you?" James wouldn't do anything to jeopardize his relationship with Will. He and Tobias would be responsible for their little brother for the rest of their lives

"No! I want another sister like Miss Becky. And Miss Cat has lots of horses. She let me ride a pretty one." Will grinned, the joy on his face evident.

James found himself smiling back. "So you think I should marry her?"

Will nodded so hard his hair flopped back and forth. "She's pretty and she wears trousers like a man."

"That she does." James loved the unblemished view of the world through Will's eyes.

"Then marry her." Will smiled. "I'll go have supper with Miss Becky and Toby. She always gives me dessert."

James pulled his brother into a hug. The simplest answer was always the right one. He just had to listen to his heart and not his foolish head.

He had a woman to convince to marry him.

Cat threw the curry brush into the bucket on the wall and called it a day. She was exhausted. After not sleeping well for a week, or bunking with the horses, she was bleary eyed. However, running herself into a stupor was the only way to stop herself from dreaming. She'd discovered James invaded her dreams.

His lips, his hands, his body, all of it echoed through her memories. She'd been waking up aroused and frustrated. When she'd shouted her displeasure, Eva had communicated her own at being woken up in the middle of the night yet again by Cat's restless sleep.

If something didn't happen soon, Cat might never sleep again. Her nieces and nephews had been looking at her oddly. Meredith went so far as to tell her she was being mean. Matt's oldest daughter, one of the twins, earned her bossiness from her father. She'd learned her directness from her Aunt Catherine.

Cat patted the gelding's neck and left the stall. It was time to stop moping and do something. What she'd do, she still didn't know. What she did know was that she missed James. Missed him so much it made her sick. She never expected to fall in love so hard.

Her musings were interrupted when she heard a noise at the back of the barn and stopped her internal whining to listen. It was suppertime, which meant no one should be in there. Except her, who was avoiding being around people.

"Matt, is that you?"

Her voice echoed through the barn. A few of the horses responded to her call, but no humans. Her hand went to her hip but there was no pistol there. She'd hung it up near the door of the barn when she'd come in.

Cat had nothing but her wits and a curry brush.

Damn.

She crept forward, keeping to the edges to avoid stepping on the straw that spilled from the stalls, which had a tendency to crinkle. Her heart thumped but she kept her calm. It could be a dog or a stray animal that had found its way into the large barn.

When she reached the corner to the back of the bar, she peered around the edge of the wood. Shadows filled the corners with patches of late-day sun squeezing in through the cracks of the wood.

Something moved to her right.

Cat turned toward the sound and straightened up, tired of hiding. Tired of being afraid to take a chance anymore. This wasn't who she was. She wasn't just someone who trained the equines on the Circle Eight. Cat was strong, intelligent and skilled with horses. Cat could use every weapon on the ranch and protect herself. She had to remember who she was, something she'd lost two weeks ago when her horses were stolen.

She grabbed a pitchfork, holding it in front of her. "All right, you son of a bitch. Come out. I'm done with this foolishness."

"I wasn't hiding." James walked toward her with a burlap sack in his hand. "I was looking for you."

At the sight of the man she loved, whom she'd been missing terribly, she got angry. It was better than brooding and feeling sorry for herself.

"What makes you think I want to see you?" She stuck out her jaw, determined to fight for what she wanted. Whatever that was.

He reached for his gun and shock held her immobile. Her mouth dropped open when he cocked and fired.

CHAPTER SEVENTEEN

James thought he might have aimed sideways, his hand shook so bad. Seeing Chino aim for Cat's head had been the most frightening moment of James's life. The gun boomed in his hand just as Chino squeezed the trigger. He fell backward, scattering loose straw in the air. The bullet slammed into a beam above him, showering Cat with pieces of wood.

She yelped and batted at the splinters. "What the hell are you doing?"

He walked toward her, his breath still not returning to his body. James saw stars as he approached her. She pointed the pitchfork at him.

"Don't come any closer."

He managed to point to the body behind her. She whirled around and dropped the pitchfork with a clang.

"Holy shit."

James dragged in a breath. "Damn right. Holy fucking shit." He walked toward her, his heart about to explode out of his chest. He'd almost lost her. What if he hadn't been there? Cat could be lying in a pool of blood instead of Chino.

That thought made him want to puke.

He made it to her side as the barn door burst open and the Graham clan tumbled in, Matt in the lead with his gun in hand.

"What the hell happened?" Matt came to a skidding halt at the body. "Son of a bitch."

"Pa, you're not supposed to cuss." Meredith had followed her father.

He scowled at her. "Get your butt back in that house, Meredith Graham, before I remind you what a whooping feels like."

She stuck her chin in the air and grunted in protest as she stomped out of the barn. She reminded James so much of Cat he almost smiled. Matt had his hands full with that one. And she was a twin. A dizzying thought.

Matt turned to Cat. "What happened?"

"I have no idea." She looked at James with confusion in her gaze. "I thought James came to kill me but he shot Chino instead."

Matt crouched beside Chino then shifted his gaze to James. "Right between the eyes. Good shot, Gibson."

He nodded, his voice still caught where he couldn't reach it. The thought of Cat being killed scared him more than anything in his life.

Hannah appeared, her brown eyes full of concern. "Cat, are you all right?"

She threw up her hands. "I don't know."

"Come inside. You've not eaten a good meal in a week." Hannah gestured to James to follow as she led Cat from the barn.

Matt and Caleb stood over the body while the rest of the family left the barn at Hannah's urging. She was good at herding unwilling children and adults. James reminded himself she was the one who'd asked him to follow Cat. Hannah was a formidable woman who had raised the blonde Graham who held his heart.

"What are you doing here?" Matt asked. "Not that I'm not grateful, considering this piece of shit almost killed my sister."

"I came to give her this." His voice was hoarse with emotion as he held up the burlap sack. "And apologize."

"Are you fixing to marry my sister, Gibson?" Caleb was showing his ex-Ranger intimidation skills.

James wasn't afraid of the brothers. Not anymore. He was afraid he might not be with Cat as he hoped.

"If she'll have me," came out of his mouth. "She's mighty stubborn so she might not say yes."

Matt crossed his arms. "All my sisters are like that. You should see them when they're together." He shook his head. "They're like an army."

James wanted to see that. He wanted to know all of the

Grahams, to become a permanent part of their lives. Their family had taught him how to love his brothers and for that he was grateful. More than that, he'd fallen in love with one of them, the woman he wanted to make his own for good.

"I don't have sisters."

"You can have mine." The corner of Matt's mouth kicked up. "If she says yes, then I don't have a choice. You've done your part to bring home the Circle Eight horses and saved Cat's life more than once. I'd say your past is wiped clean."

James let out the breath he'd been holding. His actions when he was fifteen had cost the Grahams a great deal. No matter that he'd been a boy, he'd been old enough to know he shouldn't have listened to Tobias. Regret had weighed heavily on his soul. Until now.

"Thank you." He shook Matt's hand and then Caleb's.

"Help us move this body behind the barn and then we need to figure out how he got away from Brody and Rooster." Matt frowned. "Slippery fucking weasel."

James set the sack down and got to work moving Chino from the barn. Fifteen minutes later, the three men washed up behind the house and used the backdoor to enter the kitchen.

With his burlap sack in hand, James was excited to see Cat, to find a moment to tell her what was in his heart. The kitchen was full of people. Children working on slates scattered around the table. Eva and Hannah were washing dishes. The one person James didn't see was the woman he'd come to woo.

Eva saw him and her gaze dropped to the sack. "Mr. Gibson. Thank you for saving *mi hija* again." She took his free hand in her won small ones. "I am so glad you were there for her."

He accepted her thanks with a smile. "Is she here?"

"She's asleep." Hannah offered.

James's courage faltered. "Oh. I, uh, have something for her." He thrust the burlap sack at Eva. "Can you see she gets this?"

As he made his goodbyes and escaped out the front door, he heard Eva ask aloud.

"Why did he bring jars of peaches?"

Sunlight streamed through the curtains, the heat raising the temperature in the room. Cat rolled over and flung off the blanket, too hot to keep sleeping. Judging by the brightness from outside, she'd slept late. Very, very late.

The previous day's events came back to her in a rush and she sat up so fast, her head spun. Chino had tried to kill her. James had been in the barn for some reason she had yet to determine, and he'd saved her life.

She had questions for him and last night she'd been so exhausted she could hardly think straight. Eva had tucked her into bed and Cat hadn't protested. Now it was at least twelve hours later.

James must've left the ranch without speaking to her. She should have stayed awake long enough, but her thoughts had been mixed up. Now everything was clear.

She loved him. She only hoped he'd been there to tell her he'd made a mistake by leaving a week earlier. To profess his undying love and ask her to marry him.

Cat snorted at her romantic foolishness and hauled herself out of bed. After washing with the tepid water in the pitcher, she reached for her trousers. Her hand hovered over the canvas fabric.

The blue dress hung on a hook beside them. The dress she'd worn for Tobias and Rebecca's wedding reminded her that she was beautiful no matter what she wore. However she knew if she wanted to fight for James, she needed to do something drastic.

She picked up the dress.

When she entered the kitchen, Eva and Hannah were at the table doing mending. The younger children were gathered in a circle in the great room while Meredith read to them. It was a peaceful scene. Too bad her stomach was jumping like a couple of frogs had taken up residence.

They all stopped to stare at her. She squirmed at being on display and had to push down her angry words. Her family wasn't to blame here. She had only worn a dress once in fifteen years. This was an occasion.

Cat managed a shaky smile and curtsied. The children clapped and she laughed with them. Eva got to her feet and took Cat's hands, spreading them wide while she looked her fill.

"Ah, *hija*, you are beautiful." Eva's dark eyes were full of pride. "How can he resist you?"

Cat made a face. "He's done a good job so far."

Hannah pointed to a burlap sack at the end of the table. "I'm not so sure about that. He left that for you last night. His face when he found out you were asleep was more than disappointed. I think he was here to ask you something."

Cat's frogs turned into herd. "That's for me?"

She approached the bag, afraid of what she would find. When she loosened the rope around the neck and peered in, she spotted three jars of peaches. A happy sob exploded from her throat.

"What is it?" Hannah reached for Cat's hand.

Cat pressed her hand to her mouth and shook her head. "He loves me."

"Of course he does. I could see that plain as day." Hannah smiled. "Go get him, Catherine."

Cat kissed both Eva and Hannah before she picked up the sack and headed for the door.

It was time to get her man.

James pushed the wheelbarrow out the back of the barn. Sweat dripped down his face but he didn't wipe it away. He needed to think about nothing but work or his thoughts would drift to Cat.

She hadn't even bothered to speak to him after he'd shot Chino. She ran and hid. Again. That told him all he needed to know. She didn't reciprocate his feelings. The time they'd spent together had been intense for both of them, but while it had only confirmed his love, it had apparently been just bodily needs for her.

That hurt. A lot.

He turned the wheelbarrow to return to the barn when a vision stepped into the doorway. James dropped the wheelbarrow and stared.

Cat stood there wearing the blue dress. *The* dress she'd been wearing when he'd realized the depths of his feelings for her. Her hair was down again, the breeze gently lifting strands to dance in the air. Her expression was serious; no smile hid behind her blue eyes.

She held up the burlap sack and his heart thumped hard. "You left this for me."

It wasn't a question. "I did."

She glanced down at it. "I'm sorry I was already in bed when you did. I haven't been sleeping the last week."

He was surprised by the confession. "Neither have I."

She returned her gaze to his. "Why?"

"Why haven't I been sleeping?" He didn't want to explain that to her. It would be far too embarrassing.

"No, why did you leave me three jars of peaches?"

Memories of sharing them, of the sweet taste of them in her mouth when he kissed her, almost made him moan aloud.

"I know you like them." He inwardly winced as the lame words left his mouth.

"Is that all?"

He nodded, unsure of what was going on. He didn't like feeling out of control, but she did it to him every time.

"I thought maybe you were telling me you loved me." Her eyes closed for a moment. "Because I really, really wanted to hear it again."

"I, uh, what?" He blinked, the earth beneath him shifting.

"I love you, James Gibson. I've loved you for more than a year, since the first time you kissed me. I was too stubborn to accept it, to confess it, and it almost cost me the most precious thing in my life." She set the bag down, stepped toward him and stopped a mere foot away. "You."

Tears stung his eyes. "What are you saying?"

That was when she smiled and all the breath whooshed from his body. "I'm saying will you marry me?"

James didn't know whether to shout at the sky or break out into a jig. "You're asking *me* to marry *you*?"

"Why not? I love you. I hope you love me. We rub along well together." She reached out and cupped his whiskered, very dirty cheek. "What do you say?"

He had to swallow the giant lump in his throat before he could force the words out. "I say you've turned me inside out, Catherine Frances Graham. You've driven me mad every moment for the last year." He took her hand and kissed the palm, cognizant of how much he stank at the moment, but he couldn't stop himself. Not again. Not ever again. "I love you and, yes, I'll marry you if you'll marry me."

Her smile was brighter than a thousand suns. "I'm glad I didn't wear this dress for nothing."

She wrapped her arms around him and her mouth found his. This kiss was more powerful than an army. Shivers and tingles raced through him. She was his. She loved him. He loved her.

James was going to marry Catherine.

CHAPTER EIGHTEEN

A month after she'd asked James to marry her, Cat woke on her wedding day. The sun wasn't up yet so she had time to go for a short ride. She'd adopted Kick as her own horse since Paladin might not ever return. It had taken time for she and the gelding to get to know each other.

She'd taken to riding in the early morning with him as she'd done for years. Sometimes Matt joined her, but he'd begun to enjoy time in bed with his wife more than a dawn ride. She didn't blame him. Cat sincerely hoped to enjoy many mornings with James in the future.

They had decided to marry in the middle of the morning, to buck tradition, and start their married life as early in the day as possible. Then they could spend more time in bed alone after a wedding breakfast.

She left the house, pleased to find a cool morning. May had arrived with the taste of summer heat but today, on the most special day of her life, the weather was perfect. She greeted Kick with a peppermint. After she'd discovered the horse's penchant for them, she made sure to bring one each day. The memory of her mother's stash of peppermints had evolved into Cat's new stash. She had to hide it from her nieces and nephews. Since there were so many of them, it wasn't easy.

With a smile she couldn't shake, she saddled Kick and led him from the barn. Her pistol rode on her hip. The experience with Chino had reminded her to always be armed and ready to defend herself.

She would ride for half an hour, without straying too far. As the sun slid up the horizon, the blood-red rays lit up the ground in front of her. She rode toward the big tree on the rise. It was a spot the Graham siblings had escaped to for years, its large branches providing shade and a place to think.

As she rode toward the tree, which provided a nice view of the horse and barn, someone stepped out from behind the trunk. Her hand slid to her hip and she cursed herself for wanting that last ride alone before her marriage.

"Cat."

Her heart slammed into her throat. "Benjy?"

She pulled Kick to a stop and slid from the saddle, running to her brother. She hugged him tight, so happy to find him alive.

"You came home."

"No. I came to see you. I heard you were getting married." His words were quiet in the early morning stillness. "I wanted to wish you the best."

She shook her head. "You have to come home. Let us help you. The Rangers know what Chino and Cunningham did. Caleb and Brody are doing their best to clear your name. If you don't come home, they can't make a good argument for you."

"I can't. There's no way I can ever come home."

"But you're so close. Please." She was desperate to help him.

"Don't ask me again. I won't change my mind." His voice was low and firm. He glanced at the horse. "You're riding Kick."

She smiled at him through teary eyes. "He's a good horse."

"So is your Paladin. He's been a good companion." Ben kissed her forehead and stepped away. "Be happy, Kitty."

"Benjy, I can't say goodbye to you again."

He sighed. "I can't come back, not after all that happened."

"Chino's dead. James killed him." She clung to his arm.

He kissed her forehead. "I have to go. I don't know if you'll see me again."

She wanted to yell at him, tell him to stop being foolish, but he was a man who made his own decisions. Cat had fought against everyone telling her what to do for more than ten years. Who was she to do the very thing she bucked against?

"Can I tell everyone I saw you?"

"No. Don't." Ben shook his head. "If they knew I was nearby they'd chase me down."

She didn't want the responsibility to keep the secret, but she would for him. "Be safe."

He squeezed her hand and then disappeared over the rise. She leaned against the tree and took a deep breath. Cat felt better knowing Ben was alive and free, but she would worry about him until he was home.

She got back on Kick and walked him back home, her enjoyment of the ride tempered by Ben's visit. Cat wouldn't betray his secret. Someday she hoped he would return.

When she reached the barn, Matt was waiting for her. Cat's cheeks flushed, as if he could read her mind and knew her secret.

"You're up early." He smiled at her. She was surprised to notice a few more gray hairs on his head. He looked so much like she remembered of Pa. In truth, Matt had been her pa longer than their father.

"I was excited." She walked Kick toward his stall. "Thought I'd get in a ride before I had to get gussied up."

As she unsaddled the horse and rubbed him down, Matt chatted with her. It was unusual to have a quiet moment with her oldest brother and she cherished it. He would be the one to give her away at the wedding and soon she and James would live in their own cabin on the Circle Eight.

Everything was about to change. Again. This time Cat was excited and looking forward to married life with James.

"Was that Ben up there?"

Cat stopped in mid-motion. She didn't respond, unwilling to lie to Matt but not knowing what to say.

"It's all right. You don't have to tell me. I was riding behind you and I saw him." Matt rubbed at his eyes. "I never thought I'd see him. I'm glad he came to see you."

Cat turned to him. "I can't betray him."

"Loyalty is always at the core of our family. When he's ready, he'll come back. At least we know he's alive." Matt's smile was sad. "Are you ready to get married, little one?"

This time her smile came easily. "Yep. And this is one dress I won't mind wearing."

He held out his arm. "Then let's get back to the women before they wake up looking for the bride."

Cat slipped her hand into the crook of his arm. "I love you, Matt."

"Love you too, Catherine." He kissed her cheek.

Cat returned to the house to prepare for her wedding. Knowing her family loved her and supported her gave her an extra boost in her step.

The rest of her life was about to begin.

James pulled on the string tie with shaking hands. He'd worn a brand new shirt Hannah had made for him, along with his best trousers. Rebecca had pressed his clothes for him the night before.

He wasn't nervous about marrying Cat. He was anxious to make her his own, but at the same time, taking the responsibility of a wife was a big one. Their cabin was freshly constructed about a mile from the main Graham house. Each of her sisters and brothers, except Ben of course, had given them their time to help construct the three-bedroom home.

They had a bed and a stove. James had been making a table and chairs as a wedding gift for Cat. He wasn't an expert at woodworking but he was proud of what he'd made for her.

"You nervous?" Tobias came in pulling at the collar of his shirt.

"Nah. I'm ready." James grinned as his brother continued to fight the dress shirt. "You know you can wear whatever you want to the wedding. I won't care."

"Rebecca would. She's going on and on about how her baby sister is becoming a woman." Tobias leaned against the doorframe. "I think she became a woman before now." He waggled his eyebrows.

"I ain't saying a word." James slicked down one unruly curl and pronounced himself ready. "We need to leave soon. Is Will ready?"

"He's playing jacks with Rebecca. He's so excited she had to calm him down." Tobias straightened. "I know things haven't been easy between us in our lives, but you and Will are my family for now and for always. I wanted you to know I'm real proud of you, little brother."

James smiled through the emotional lump in his throat and held out his hand. "That means a lot."

Tobias waved the extended hand and pulled James into a

quick hug. "I wish you nothing but the best."

James hadn't always seen eye to eye with his older brother, but he wouldn't trade his family for anything. He gestured to the door.

"After you. I'm ready to claim my bride."

The blue sky and bright sunshine brought the perfect day to get married. The same preacher who had married Tobias and Rebecca had come from Houston to perform the ceremony. Not quite a year later, he was still the round, bald and friendly man who was a friend of Elizabeth and Vaughn's.

As Cat walked out of the house on Matt's arm toward her future, she trembled. Matt leaned toward her.

"Are you fixing to run off on me?"

She laughed. "No, I'm ready to get married."

She didn't shake from fear or nervousness. The entire of her family, minus Ben, plus James's family had come together for the wedding. The love and joy almost shimmered on the air.

"Do you think Mama and Pa would be proud of me?" she blurted as they crossed the yard.

"I think they're always with us and they'd be busting their buttons with pride. You're the best horse trainer in the state of Texas, Catherine. No matter what, your family loves you. I know I'm gonna be foolish today over you." Matt squeezed her arm. "You're my baby sister. I taught you how to saddle a horse, how to tie a knot, hell, I taught you how to wash dishes."

She laughed. "We're very blessed, Matt."

"We sure are."

They reached the side of the house where everyone waited. All the faces turned toward them and she smiled so hard, her cheeks hurt. Her gaze, however, was only on one person. The man who held her heart.

He was handsome in his new shirt and pressed trousers. The love she had for this man was endless. Catherine walked toward him, toward the future, with the knowledge she had found the mate she'd always dreamed of.

Love had come to the Circle Eight once again.

<<<◇>>>

ABOUT THE AUTHOR

Beth Williamson, who also writes as Emma Lang, is an award-winning, New York Times and USA Today bestselling author of both historical and contemporary romances. Her books range from sensual to scorching hot. She is a Career Achievement Award Nominee in Erotic Romance by Romantic Times Magazine, in both 2009 and 2010, and a semi-finalist in the 2014 Amazon Breakthrough Novel Award Contest.

Beth has always been a dreamer, never able to escape her imagination. It led her to the craft of writing romance novels, fueled by Reese's and tenacious pursuit of the perfect story. She's passionate about purple, books, and her family. She has a weakness for shoes and purses as well as bookstores.

Life might be chaotic, as life usually is, but Beth always keeps a smile on her face, a song in her heart, and a cowboy on her mind. ;)

Website: www.bethwilliamson.com
Facebook: www.facebook.com/bethwilliamson
Twitter: www.twitter.com/authorbethw
Newsletter: http://eepurl.com/fd822

Circle Eight series:
http://www.bethwilliamson.com/series/circle-eight/

CPSIA information can be obtained at www.ICGtesting.com
Printed in the USA
LVOW07s0210120915

453919LV00006B/700/P